D0369959

SEND MORE TOURISTS...
THE LAST ONES WERE DELICIOUS

SEND MORE
TOURISTS,
THE LAST
ONES
WERE
DELIC

J M C P L
DISCARDED

TRACEY WADDLETON

IOUS.

BREAKWATER
P.O. BOX 2188, ST. JOHN'S, NL, CANADA, A1C 6E6
WWW.BREAKWATERBOOKS.COM

COPYRIGHT © 2019 Tracey Waddleton

All of the characters and events portrayed in this book are fictitious.
Any resemblance to actual persons, living or deceased, is purely
coincidental.

ISBN 978-1-55081-780-5

A CIP catalogue record for this book is available from Library
and Archives Canada

ALL RIGHTS RESERVED. No part of this publication may be
reproduced, stored in a retrieval system or transmitted, in any
form or by any means, without the prior written consent of the
publisher or a licence from The Canadian Copyright Licensing
Agency (Access Copyright). For an Access Copyright licence,
visit www.accesscopyright.ca or call toll free to 1-800-893-5777.

We acknowledge the support of the Canada Council for the Arts.
We acknowledge the financial support of the Government
of Canada and the Government of Newfoundland and Labrador
through the Department of Tourism, Culture, Industry and
Innovation for our publishing activities.
PRINTED AND BOUND IN CANADA.

Breakwater Books is committed to choosing papers and materials
for our books that help to protect our environment. To this end,
this book is printed on a recycled paper and other controlled
sources that are certified by the Forest Stewardship Council®.

MIX
Paper from
responsible sources
FSC
www.fsc.org
FSC® C103567

FOR MICHAEL WADDLETON

• • •

CONTENTS

CONTENTS

IT LUNGED

IT LUNGED

IT LUNGED

I KNOW YOU'RE DOWN THERE.

Oh.

It slid out from under the bed and sat in the rocking chair. It was brown and blackish red and greenish purple, all at once. She thought it might eat her.

I am so lonely, it said.

But you have me, she said.

Well, until just now I wasn't sure.

She left where she'd been crouched, near her pillow. In the closet she found a small doll, a girl with hair in braids that she didn't play with anymore. She laid it on the floor between them, not getting too close.

Here, she said. This will help. And she went around the bed and climbed back in and pulled the comforter up. It reached for the doll with sticky hands, like a frog's hands. It looked the doll over. It got stuck in its hair. It rocked back and forth in the chair, humming like a mom.

How did you find me out? it asked.

It was the crying.

Oh, it said. It held the doll and twisted its hair some more. It looked nervous. It was grosser than she'd thought. It had too many feet.

I got all As, she said.

What's that?

At school, she said. I got all As. An A in drawing. An A in writing.

It stared. It said it didn't have school. What was that? It said it didn't know what these were: drawing and writing. What was an A? Then it started to wail again. It trembled, its muscles bulging. Things like tears shot from its mass. The little girl held her pillow like a shield. She remembered how it had once jumped out at her, grabbed her ankle with claws. How she had screamed. It looked up and laughed. Then it said it was sorry.

I'm sorry, too.

It shook its head. For what? it asked.

That you don't have school or drawing, writing. That you are sad.

The doll had hair that was all matted now. She wouldn't have wanted it back, even if it offered.

Where are you from? she asked.

From here.

From *here* here?

Oh, yes. From here. Well, under there, it said and pointed to the bed, where the girl was sitting.

I'd like it best if you didn't go back, she said, and this started it crying again. When you grab me, it's scary.

Well, but it's my job. Mostly.

Mostly?

Yes.

What else do you do?

I hide in the closet, try to frighten your mother when she is hanging up your clothes. She doesn't see me.

Oh, the little girl said.

I wanted more, it said. It stood and fanned, its tentacles scraping the wall.

The phone buzzed, blinked red light.

That's just my phone, she said. I sent a text.

What's that?

It's just a message, she said. I texted Dad to come downstairs, that there was a monster.

I figured that, the monster grinned, so I locked the door.

It lunged.

OLD BEN WALSH

OLD BEN WALSH

OLD BEN WALSH

HOW IT WAS TOLD WAS that Ben Walsh took Millie out behind the breakwater and did it to her there. He was a dirty old man, Ben Walsh. Everybody knew that.

People were talking, so Mom kept Millie out of school for a week. Danny Oldfried came to my table at lunch and asked if my sister was a slut now, could he have a go at her, so I punched him in the nose and spent the next period in the principal's office.

I understand, Mrs. Jenkins said, that this is a sensitive issue, so we won't call your parents. Go on back to class, she said.

When I got home, I walked right into Millie's room where she was sitting listening to records, day five on the pip. I said, do you know what people are saying, and she didn't so much as turn her head, so I slammed the door and went to my room. I lay on the bed with my shoes still on and I thought about Danny Oldfried's father out shearing sheep in their yard, about this one time my father bought a lamb from him, how Dad walked to the barn while we waited in the car and how the lamb bleated before they slit its throat, the shrill yelp slicing through the car window. Millie with her hands over her ears, bawling in the car seat.

When Millie came back to school, she looked right different: smaller. Mom started trying to walk us down to the bus stop and I had to tell her to go on, not to be mental about it. She kept glancing back at us as she made her way home. Go on, b'y, I yelled, and so she finally turned and went, leaving us there, Millie in headphones.

Millie was called into the counselor's office, made a big fuss over. The counselor was a woman from St. John's with a degree in psychology, liked getting in people's business. It was said she told everything in the teachers' lounge afterwards. She kept Millie in there all morning, and at lunch time, Millie sat by herself instead of with her friends, Josie Gordon and Lana O'Neill. Some important now, they said. Josie said it's too bad Ben Walsh didn't have a go at *her* so she could miss class all morning, too. Later that afternoon, that saucy old Clara White asked Millie in the bathroom if she'd had her cherry popped and Millie didn't say anything at all, apparently. Just stood there gawking at herself in the mirror, like an idiot.

After school, the boys were all around her, picking at her skirt and her hair. One of the teachers watched and said to get out of it, to leave her alone, but the boys started up again as soon as the bus was pulling away. Millie didn't say a thing, not even when Pete Smith tried to put his hand on her tit. She just stuck her hands under her armpits and looked out the window. I told Mom all about it and that was some way to be getting on, don't ya think? Mom told me to leave it alone, that it was none of my goddamned business, and to set the table for supper. Dad said not to mind it. Women were funny creatures.

I heard them talking one night through their window when I was sneaking a smoke out mine.

How are we going to get through this? Dad asked.

It's no odds, Mom said, to anybody else what's going on in this house.

I s'ppose, he said.

Ah, pretty soon they'll be onto their next target, Mom said, and shut down the conversation or else caught on to my smoking, so I closed the window and killed the light.

Mom tried talking to Millie. She went to the store and bought her presents like nail polishes and shampoos and other things. She brought them home and knocked on Millie's door and they'd talk in the room with the door closed, then Mom would come out, dejected, and tell me to go on, get out of there. Millie started locking her door eventually. She didn't eat at dinner and sometimes wandered off from the table. Sometimes Dad let her go. Other times he hauled her back by the arms, sat her in her chair and pushed her head at the plate of food. She'd sit with her head bent like that for the rest of the meal, and after a while, he'd swipe the plate from under her face and eat it all himself. Some waste, he would say to Mom on the days when he couldn't eat both dinners, but Mom kept on setting the table for Millie every evening all the same.

Millie got blasting her music, too. Weird depressing stuff she got from these older kids she'd started hanging with. They picked her up in this old Crown Vic, these greasy boys, far from the house so my parents wouldn't see. I had half a mind to rat her out, but you don't do that kind of thing, even when it might be called for.

Our older cousin Justin said it to me at a party one night that we should go after them young fellas. Millie was in the corner making out with Jordan Casper, and he was alright, he was on the hockey team. I didn't like him pawing my sister like that, but at least it wasn't one of those weird kids she was in with.

Yeah, I said, Let's do it.

Millie's report card came back with Ds, and Mom and Dad threw a fit in the living room. I went out for a drive. When I came back, the house was right quiet and the lights were off. Mom left a plate of dinner for me in the fridge. I waited in the silence. It was only nine o'clock. I carried the plate to my room, the dog padding along behind me like he was freaked out too, and I thought I heard Millie sniffling, but I didn't go in.

Me and Justin found those grease balls down by the river with a couple of girls in their car. I marched right up to them and told them to stay away from my sister, that she was already fucked up enough after what happened, and they just laughed. Justin grabbed the driver, Billy Molloy, by the collar and Billy didn't look like he minded at all, just turned up the heavy metal and starting head-banging.

They're cultured, Justin said. Fucking bunch from the tracks.

Yeah, fuck them, I said but Millie was out driving around with them the next afternoon, giving me the finger as they sped off from the hangout.

By December, there was a social worker coming round the house from over in Placentia. She showed up unannounced sometimes. Mom said it was like being under surveillance. She was afraid to have a dirty dish in the sink. They take your youngsters for nothing, she'd heard. Mrs. White said not to worry, that she was a good mother and a good housekeeper and it was pretty standard after news got around about Millie and Ben Walsh.

Don't worry, Mrs. White said, lots of that stuff went on over the years and there was nothing to be done but to go on with things.

On the weekends, I'd knock on Millie's door, have a couple of beer before we'd go out. We'd drink and listen to music. It became our thing to do on Friday and Saturday nights, me sat on the side of her bed getting primed before the b'ys came to get me. I tried talking to her about school. I tried talking to her about the silly music she was listening to. Get out of that, Millie, I'd say. That stuff'll drive you to off yourself. And she'd just laugh.

Sometimes she showed up later at the lake, with Brian Critch or Johnny Tobin, that crowd. Draped over them, face full of makeup. Then we wouldn't talk. She wouldn't even look my way.

One of these Friday nights I went to her room and she was in some kind of mood. Go, she said, before I could even sit down. Go, she said, and kept her back to me, and she didn't turn when I asked why. I waited another few minutes before leaving the two Molson Ice I'd smuggled in for her, and that was the end of those visits.

I got a bump up on the hockey team that winter and started going out with Mary Anne Hennebury. Mary

Anne was a hard girl to get your hands on. I picked her up on the bike and took her to the woods a few times and I was careful not to touch her, just hung out and skimmed rocks on the lake and listened to her go on about Boone's Geography class. She told me how hard it was and could I help her study and sure, I said, but I didn't let on that the reason for my marks was that I'd been helping Chris Dunnegan steal the tests all semester. They'd said Mary Anne was frigid, but on the third night at her house after studying, we were watching movies in the rec room and she let me finger her pussy. By March we were at it like rabbits. Being with Mary Anne was like living in a cloud. We went to all the dances, everybody envied me for having her, and somehow I forgot all about Millie. Then she went and burnt down father's shed.

I was giving it to Mary Anne on her rec room couch when the phone rang and her mother yelled from upstairs it's your father, b'y, and I got some fright. I got home just as the fire truck was pulling away. Dad was standing on the front lawn talking to the cops and Millie was in the back seat of a cruiser, looking right proud of herself.

All destroyed, Dad was saying. Tools and Christmas decorations. Old family albums. Jesus, he was saying. Jesus! And getting right worked up like that. The officer kept putting his hand on his shoulder.

It's too bad, Mr. Whalen, he said, townie accent. That's for sure. How old did you say your daughter was?

I found Mom in the kitchen standing over a sink full of dishes, worrying her hands over a dishcloth. The shed sat in the back, a black hulk of ash and wood, a bit of foundation was all that was left.

She's gone too far this time, Tommy, was all Mom said, and she twisted the cloth back and forth in her hands, like readying rope for a beating.

It was real quiet around the house for the next few days. Millie was still at the lockup, Mom and Dad trying to decide what to do with her. She was off the rails, I heard them saying. The social worker came for tea and Mom was relieved this time. They had a big chat and I slipped off to Mary Anne's, slept there for the night.

Millie was let out after one night. She went to her room and shut and locked the door, and I sat outside on the deck, smoking and drinking one of Dad's beer. There was some racket. Uncle Mitch came over carrying a 12-gauge. I'd seen the gun before. Grandpa left it to him. It was long and shiny, wood casing with a black barrel.

Go, Dad said, when he saw me coming down toward them, so I went back to the house. In the kitchen, a few women—Mrs. White, and the lady from church, the minister's wife—sat at the table and looked on my mother, who was still in a state from the argument. Mrs. Henry stirred a pot on the stove and somebody put a tape on, turned the volume up a bit loud.

No, Mom said. Jesus, no.

Have a drink, they said, and poured her something amber from an unmarked bottle.

I walked up the stairs to my room. Millie's door lay open but she wasn't in there. I lay on the bed with my shoes still on and I thought about Mary Anne and that skirt she was wearing at school and I must have been drifting off when the first shot sounded because it was half-muffled, far away like. The second one was sharp, clear as a bell as I was tearing down the stairs. I could hear Mom wailing in the kitchen. One of the women caught me by the shirt collar just as I was getting to the back door, and hauled me back.

Sure, there was nothing to be done, she said and set the kettle on the stove.

TWO FOR JOY

TWO FOR JOY

TWO FOR JOY

IT'S THE SUMMER THE CROWS terrorize Harvey Road. The paper runs five stories in a two-week period. Jake thinks the whole thing is too much. *Generous* is the word he uses.

One night in August, Emma caught him on the porch with his pellet gun and coaxed him inside. She was wearing one of those flimsy cotton dresses, the kind with a row of buttons that run all down the middle. He pulled her into his arms and led her in a little dance, right in front of the neighbours. But that was before. Today it's the cool dart of a fall wind as he and Bob wait at the drive-thru window.

Three dollars and forty-two cents. Is that what she said? Bob is squirming, hands deep in his pockets, beer belly pulling the seatbelt. The papers on the dash come fluttering to his lap. He hauls out two dimes.

Christ, he says.

It's okay. I've got it.

Are you sure?

Not a problem, bud.

The girl at the drive-thru is no more than seventeen, all tits and blonde hair. Jake hands her his credit card.

Wouldn't mind a bit of that to throw around, if you know what I mean, Bob snorts as they pull onto the road.

Something by Roy Orbison is on the radio. Jake flicks the channel to the campus station where it's static and punk and it's about here that he catches a glimpse of her, on the other side of the street, stepping onto a bus. At least, he thinks it's her.

Emma.

Hair in a loose bun, shit-kicking leather boots and leggings, a sweater to her knees. That face of hers. And then she's gone again, down a flight of stairs, and the red light goes green. Jake hits the gas a little too hard and the SUV lurches forward. Bob's coffee splashes onto his shirt, his crotch.

Fuck!

Watch the upholstery, b'y!

What about third-degree burns, motherfucker? Why don't you watch the third-degree fucking burns?

How about I buy you another coffee?

How about *fuck you*?

The house is quiet when they arrive, like it's supposed to be. The key turns the same in the lock.

You made this, didn't you? Bob runs a hand over the stair rails. You should haul it out and take it with you.

He lingers there at the bottom of the steps while Jake pulls a suitcase from the hallway closet.

It only takes them an hour. Jake leaves most of the tools, except for a small kit and a few things Bob asks for.

He packs the car and takes one last look around the house and then the shed, where he finds the gun and the little tin can full of pellets he bought earlier the summer.

Out on the balcony, you can just see the nest, high among a gathering of firs in front of the cathedral. Jake turns the lid of the little tin can carefully. He takes out three pellets, and pushes the first one into the gun's splintering wood.

Careful, now, Bob says, it's easy to…

The first pellet releases with a pop. High in the trees, the nest shakes and stops.

Jake inserts another pellet, fires again. Beside him, Bob is dancing excitedly. The nest is hit and falls to the side, hanging by a twig.

Not sure if three will do it. That's a pretty crazy shot. Mind if I have a go? Bob asks, but Jake rings off a third shot quickly, and the nest is loosed from its perch and falls to the bushes below. When they reach it, they find two adult birds, bloody from the assault. One is writhing, still alive, working its beak. Jake cracks its neck.

Bob walks to a garbage bin to tip out the last of his coffee, sending cream and sugar all down the sides. Out crawl the yellowjackets, four or five of them. One flies into Jake's face, hovers there a minute, looking at him. Jake wonders if it's worried.

He throws the rifle over his shoulder and they head back to the truck, the crows heavy and wet at the bottom of the bag.

• • •

There is a fine for firing a weapon inside city limits and a charge for killing the crows. The article doesn't mention Jake's name and the officers at the door are friendly and forgiving but Bob still yells fuck off from the kitchen and the b'ys all laugh.

Thanks, Jake says, and reclaims his beer.

When is it? Bob asks. He is wearing the same blue jogging pants he slept in the past two nights.

October 19th.

Don't you even worry about it, Cliff says. I know a guy in Wildlife.

This isn't Wildlife, Jake says. This is the cops.

Wildlife can fix any problem, Cliff says and the rest of them nod their heads like it's gospel truth.

They lay the table for poker and then Bob gets them to go upstairs and stand around the computer so he can show them what he's talking about. One of his neighbours has posted topless pictures on the internet. Bob found them innocently enough, but he's been messaging her for two months now, saying he's a guy from Texas. Bob from Texas. She says she's going to send him something even more racy, Bob tells them. He doesn't think her husband knows.

It's like a fucking soap opera, Ken says.

Fucking suburbs, Cliff says.

The game is a blur of drunk. Cliff takes them for all they're worth. Jake loses two hundred dollars and has to sign a note promising three dozen beer. Cliff and Ken are gone by midnight, peeling off in an F150. Jake wonders what she's doing. Emma on a Friday night.

Bob makes up the couch and, being Bob, he doesn't ask how many more nights. He takes the creaking stairs to his room and Jake listens to him mucking about up there for a while, trying hard not to wonder what he's at on webcam.

• • •

Crow. Raven. War bird. Carrier of souls. National bird of Bhutan, wherever that is. It is said they can tell one human face from another.

You look awful, she says.

Jake can't speak.

What are you doing to yourself, Jake?

Her eyes are green.

Jake wakes in a sweat, the television still muttering in the corner. He reaches for one of Bob's cigarettes and lights it before thinking. When he can't stop coughing, Bob yells from upstairs, What's the matter, b'y?

Nothing, Jake says and go on back to bed, and he puts the cigarette out and when he opens his eyes Bob is standing over him, saying it's time for work.

It's some other kid at the drive-thru, no tits, hair black and slick. When they pass the house, Jake doesn't look because Bob is watching him to see if he will. They're at the site an hour and Bob is into it with the foreman.

Stop, the foreman is yelling, coming at Bob with his hands in the air. Bob has backed the truck too far up on the lawn and he's still coming, radio blaring. The foreman jumps aside so the tire misses his foot and he reaches in and grabs Bob by the neck through the window.

Jesus Christ, b'y! You're gonna kill somebody.

Sorry, boss, Bob says and puts the brakes on.

Get this truck off the lawn!

Oh, sure thing, boss! Bob says, and then he's tumbling out over the sidewalk, narrowly missing the parked cars.

Hard-ass, he says a few minutes later when they're hauling sod. Sure, we got enough grass to fix it, don't we?

He pats Jake on the back and it's this that Jake likes most about Bob: he's optimistic to the point of jail time.

October 19th, Jake remembers.

• • •

I think he did the right thing, the caller from Clarenville says. Sure, they were attacking people.

I'm not sure anybody was attacked.

Well, people had to alter their routes to work and everything. I think he did the right thing, she says, and he says thank you, next caller.

After supper, Jake goes for a jog on the trails.

What are you going at that for? Bob says, smirking, same blue jogging pants, from the doorway.

The streetlights are switching on, dim in the misty dark. Jake tries to meditate on the crunch of his sneakers. When that doesn't work, he puts in earphones and keeps pace to the music. A mix of songs Emma made when they got their gym memberships. He could go to the gym, he realizes. She could be there, working out her frustrations on an elliptical. He could act like he's there to exercise. Pretend he doesn't notice her.

He ups his pace, near sprints, and counts out half a kilometre before he has to stop and lean on a light post to catch his breath. Overhead, he hears them cawing and when he looks up there are three.

One for sorrow. Two for joy. Three for a girl. They are saying, look, it's him. The killer of crows.

• • •

They might as well be in a foreign land, but somehow Bob is thriving. He insisted on George Street, this dance bar full of twenty year olds. He's not so bad off in jeans and a black silk shirt. Jake sips his beer. Ken and his wife are beside him at the bar, whispering.

I'm going to dance! Bob yells.

What?

I'm going to dance! He says again, and he does a little pelvic thrust and winks, then bounds off after a couple of college girls he's been plying with Rev for the better part of the evening. He is comical, a jester. There is one girl behind him and one ahead—a girl sandwich, he will say later—and he is pointing down at their heads as if to say, holy shit, and he is unbelieving, all smiles. Jake laughs and Ken and Suzy laugh, and so many of the drinks on the bar glow blue in the black light.

In the wee hours, Ken and Suzy gone for home, when Bob is waltzing on a near empty dance floor, face to chest with some bleached-blonde cougar, the redhead approaches Jake.

Can I buy you a drink? she asks and sits on the next stool, close so their arms are touching.

Emma, he says.

Marilyn, she corrects.

Oh, he says. Marilyn.

Whatever he's having, she tells the bartender.

Construction, he says when she asks what he does. Some landscaping.

Renting, he says, and thinks of the house and the sawdust that took forever to scrape from the corners of the cabinets and they're beautiful, Emma had said, and wrapped her arms around him and they boiled spaghetti on the new stove.

Car? asks the redhead.

Truck, he says.

Hmm. She is nodding, deciding his worth and he wonders if she'll tell him and put him out of his misery once and for all.

• • •

Jake wears his best suit and speaks slowly like he was told, no need for an attorney. It's a near empty courtroom. There's one lady from *The Telegram* and a woman representing a local animal-rights group who reads aloud a statement on behalf of Emma and Tom—that's what they've named them, the crows, to humanize them. They couldn't have known.

They read the charges and Jake does his best to explain. Concern for the neighbourhood, small animals and children. He tells them he meant no harm and out around the bay, where he was raised, it would have been a matter of keeping things safe, no uprising.

The fine is $200 and a mandatory firearms course. Bob high-fives him when they get back to the truck.

Tim Hortons, man, Bob says. I want to ask that girl out.

It's too cold for the wasps now. They did their slow

stupid waltz and died. They'll be back in force next year, the papers say.

The blonde is at the drive-thru window, and Bob is leaning across Jake's lap to talk to her. He is attempting to charm her with the story of Jake's court victory, but you can see she sides with the birds. The bus pulls up across the street, and she is there.

Emma.

Walking her walk down Harvey Road, shit-kicking boots and a portfolio twice the size of her, all wrapped up in a scarf, winter mitts. Her hair is long and dark and flows and rises in the waves of wind.

And he sees now that this will always be like this. That this is now the way of things.

C'mon, Bob says. What's the holdup?

Jake feels a jab in his side. Bob has his coffee held out for him to take, the drive-thru window is closed.

Got her number, Bob says. Can you believe it?

No, Jake says and he guns the engine as they leave the parking lot and head for home.

MARTHA RIDES
THE BUS AT THREE

MARTHA RIDES THE BUS AT THREE

MARTHA WILL RIDE THE BUS at three. She waits at the stop.

Step on the bus and take a seat. Don't think that the bus could crash. Don't think that the bus could stop and there will be some reason they won't let you out and you will all be sharing the same oxygen and sweating and what if you need to pee and there will be nowhere to pee, of course there will be nowhere, it's a city bus.

The doors open and Martha steps up and she pays the bus driver in quarters and he has tattoos on his knuckles.

Martha never liked motors and she doesn't like them now. Hear how they broil in the sun, lugging on. Not to be trusted. Could get your hand caught. The bus driver peeks in the mirror. He should have his eyes on the road. Probably he fixes the motors himself at the bus depot. Probably they're all doing that, unqualified. They'll break down for sure, someday. Martha should phone about it when she gets home.

In the seat ahead, two boys are chatting loudly and playing some video game. She thinks she hears the word "murder." One of the boys looks back at her and then the two of them laugh together. Perhaps she should get off at the second-last stop. Perhaps stepping out of the bus near the McDonald's would be the best thing, safer. Perhaps these boys would follow anyway and knock her down in broad daylight, take the purse and the few dollars and leave it strewn about on the sidewalk and they'll see her pills for arthritis and nobody will help her and it will be on the six o'clock news next to the story about drive-by shootings.

Imagine. Shootings in subdivisions. Fire bombings. What next?

Put the pills in your pocket and get off in front of the church and nobody will attack in front of a church, and she should have stayed home after all, and all the songs on the radio sound the same and anyway the church is coming up now.

There it goes, spinning past.

What's the point of a non-denominational service? The sign says regular service, too. Whatever that is, regular.

Her pantyhose itch at the right knee.

The boys shift and mutter and one looks back again and Martha rings the bell and steps onto the sidewalk in front of the McDonald's and the bus goes on and she has to walk an extra block to 334.

It's a nice day. It's a sunny day. There are cars on the road. There are people in cars.

Look, there is the office.

Take your time in the parking lot. Do not think about falling or you will fall. Here, you're at the door. Give the receptionist your coat. Take a seat away from the children. Read your book.

The doctor will say how are we today, Ms. Janes, and you'll say fine.

A PERSON OF CHASTITY
AND CORRECT HABITS

A PERSON OF CHASTITY
AND CORRECT HABITS

WALTON'S SMOKE SHOP OPENED AT nine on weekdays and ten on Saturdays and Sundays and Mary Moore worked five shifts a week. Each month, Mr. Walton tacked the schedule to the bulletin board behind the counter, right next to the shop's bathroom cleaning log and just above the Rules for Good Employees which started with *A smile from ear to ear.* Mr. Walton thought the world of Mary. If Mary had an appointment, she could take as much time as she needed. Every Christmas, Mr. Walton gave Mary a box of chocolates wrapped in foil paper and tied with a bow with a card attached that thanked her for her loyal dedication. So it was understandable that when Mary Moore was found floating in the duck pond behind the shop, Mr. Walton was quite beside himself.

That Monday morning, she reported to work at fifteen minutes before nine. She selected a package of Slim Donnas, regular, from one of the shelves and wrote it down as a debt to her cheque to be taken the Friday next. Mr. Walton was good about this kind of thing. More than that, Mr. Walton loved smoking. In an age where smoking was frowned upon, Mr. Walton felt it was his duty to support the dying pastime.

Mary Moore peeled the plastic wrap off the package of cigarettes and removed the insert card with the government-mandated warnings. She pulled out a Slim Donna and held it between her teeth while she searched for matches in the pocket of her blue wool coat. Mr. Walton finished his morning business just as she got the third match to light. He put on his cap and the loose bell on the door announced his departure to the crisp morning.

You have a lovely day, Miss Mary, he said, and she nodded and said, you too, sir.

• • •

Mary was a small girl and slim and pretty, drawing the attention of boys and men alike. Being pretty had its advantages. Mary always got to stand at the front of the class for photos and she won the Little Miss Dayton pageant in Grade 1. In Grade 7, she posed on the cover of the school newspaper in the new uniform for junior girls. It was her first, and last, modelling job.

She had one brother, Doug, who was two years older and could be categorized, to use the term of Mary's Uncle Dave, as retarded. Uncle Dave wasn't much for conformity. He used that word all over the place, willy-nilly like. He said it at the table when he came for supper with Doug sitting right there drooling into his peas. Look at that kid, he'd say. He's so retarded. And because of the way families were back then, and how it was easier to look the other way, Mary's parents said nothing and just went on eating.

Doug had brain damage from an improper delivery. He'd never been right. As a result, Mary's mother had quit her job as a teacher and stayed with the boy in the house day after goddamned day and when Mary was just old enough, her parents tasked her with a weekly Saturday babysitting commitment. They would pay her twenty dollars and lengthen her curfew by one hour on the other nights of the week. Please, they begged. We need a break.

What was worst about Doug was that he screamed. Sometimes he just stopped what he was doing and his head snapped back so he faced the ceiling and his mouth unhinged and widened and a great scream issued from somewhere deep within him, unprovoked. It was the kind of scream that unnerved the neighbours four houses down and sent children running for their mothers. It was loud and tangy, with a growling undertone.

If this happened when Mary's parents were home, and it happened regularly, they could sedate him with the special needle they kept locked in the dining hutch. If Mary was alone with Doug on a Saturday and the screaming started, she had her parents' permission to tie the soft scarf around his mouth to muffle the noise and stop the neighbours from calling the cops. This wasn't easy. Doug was a biter. Often Mary just turned the music loud while Doug sat on the couch and wailed like he was being murdered. Sometimes it drove her nearly mad and she ran to her closet and sat in the dresses with her hands over her ears.

Mary attended Holy Brother of the Redeemer on High Secondary School on the other side of town, far from her house and the ever-present screaming Doug. At HBRH she had a whole other life. She had friends and sometimes a boyfriend. She was president of the yearbook committee. After school, she volunteered at the animal shelter and at the church helping with the preparation of song sheets for the Sunday service. Father Ricardo thought the world of Mary Moore. He often said Mary Moore was a person of chastity and correct habits. She was thanked in the church's annual Christmas newsletter each year without fail.

When she was not volunteering or studying, she cut herself in the bathroom with her father's razor blades, dragging wide swaths across the tops of her thighs and watching the blood pearl on her cream-white skin. A drop sometimes hit the floor and formed a picture, like an ink blot. Mary wondered on the patterns of the blots. She stood and thought of what each one might represent as she applied peroxide and Band-Aids to the new wounds. Eventually, she began to see things. A windstorm was coming. She was going to fail the Civics final. Bobby was going to break up with her on Tuesday at recess.

Mary read blood like most people read tea leaves. And Bobby did break up with her at recess on a Tuesday, but just before that, he had given her a drag off his Marlboro Light on the footpath behind the old store. Something happened on the first inhale. It was like all of Mary's senses opened up. She was aware somehow. She was alive. And when Bobby said he couldn't see her anymore, she paid Tammy Munro a dollar for three cigarettes and smoked them one after the other behind the football field after the last bell rang.

At sixteen, her father left. He packed two bags in the morning and put them in the trunk of his car. Her mother cried in the driveway while Mary and Doug watched through the living-room curtain. Her mother took off her wedding ring and flushed it down the ground-floor toilet. Mr. Walton hired her the very next week, and two years later, he made her a permanent employee with benefits and everything. Each Saturday evening, she took her mother out for supper and a movie and Nurse Tilly came to sit with Doug and administer his medications, as required.

• • •

Dr. Jackson stood looking at the scars on Mary Moore's thighs and sighed. Cutters scared him. He never would have suspected Mary Moore. He told the coroner not to write it in, to spare the family. He gave the report to Mary Moore's mother personally at the door of the house that evening. Blunt force trauma. No sign of sexual assault.

Murder, Mrs. Moore whispered, and Dr. Jackson put a hand on her shoulder. She invited him in for cake and casserole. The house was teeming with food and mourners.

The first suspect to be interviewed was Mr. Walton, who had found the body. Mr. Walton arrived at work on Tuesday and found the door to the smoke shop unlocked. Immediately, the hair stood up on the back of his neck. It was so unlike Mary to do a thing like that.

Was Mary a good employee?

The best, Mr. Walton said. The absolute best.

He started sobbing and the interviewer stopped the tape and stepped out of the room and Mr. Walton had the first panic attack of his life. His throat drew closed and sweat sprouted from his forehead. He shook and shuddered and could not get control of himself at all. The event was too much for Mr. Walton's heart which quickened and clutched and stopped and Mr. Walton, beloved local proprietor of Walton's Smoke Shop, died on the carpeted floor of the police department interview room. The last image he saw was Mary Moore in her pretty blue coat standing with her Slim Donnas on the side of the building that Monday morning. The last thing he heard was the investigators rushing the room, yelling call an ambulance, suspect in distress. The ownership of the store transferred to his son, who never took one step into the smoke shop and sold it immediately to an interested party from a large chain. When the new manager took up his post some months later, he found Mary Moore's blue wool coat in the back room. He sent it to Goodwill with the rest of the unclaimed items.

The police picked up Mary Moore's fiancée, Jeff Crane. Jeff worked as a junior agent at a local real-estate firm and was top in sales in his division. He was distraught over the loss of his one true love. He could not provide an alibi for the night in question, claiming to have been at home watching a hockey game. The fact that he said he went to bed at 9:30 alarmed the investigators because of his age, but they had no evidence and so could not hold him. He was never in his lifetime relieved of the suspicion that he had done away with Mary Moore.

Suspect Three was Farlee Ellison, one of the frequenters of the smoke shop where Mary Moore had worked for four years selling cigarettes and sundries. He worked in construction and stopped into the shop once, sometimes twice, a day. He was among a group of men the other workers nicknamed The Mary Stalkers, who stood around and gawked and offered Mary gifts and told her jokes. Farlee often purchased two chocolate bars along with his Pall Malls and left the second bar on the counter for Mary. When questioned by police, he was unable to remember the night of the murder because he had been drinking. None of his favourite pubs had record of him running a tab that evening and he lived alone with his cat in a bedsitting room, where nobody tracked his movements. The other men who frequented the shop blamed Farlee for the murder and so he lost his friends and was driven to quit smoking, once and for all.

Other lesser threats were examined and dismissed in quick succession. The coat and hat shops Mary frequented said she came in regularly after receiving her pay and purchased sale items and ordered from the catalogue; that she was a lovely girl and quiet and mild. The seniors' home she visited weekly and the animal shelter where she had volunteered since high school reported no odd behavior or strange altercations involving Mary Moore in the weeks before her untimely demise.

The police investigation lasted nine months and three weeks and then was shelved due to insufficient evidence. Mrs. Moore had an angel statue erected at the head of Mary's gravesite shortly after she received the insurance payout and cashed in Mary's RRSPs. She used the remainder of the money to put Doug in a care home for the especially disabled and spent the remainder of her winters in Florida with a toy poodle named Bubsers.

• • •

On her last Monday at Walton's Smoke Shop, Mary Moore closed the store at four o'clock sharp. She counted the cash in the register and placed the float in the safe in Mr. Walton's office out back. She wiped down the counters and restocked the cigarettes, then took the day's debris to the back trash bins, propping the fire door open with a brick. Behind Walton's was a small duck pond that very few visited. One duck paddled aimlessly across it now and Mary ran back inside to get some duck feed from the fridge. She thought she heard the bell on the shop door ring, but then it was silent, and besides, she remembered, she'd locked the door.

Dark was falling as Mary crouched by the pond and held her hand out for the little duck. He seemed lonely and lost. He ate ferociously out of her palm. While she watched him, she got a funny sensation in her head, like her brain was jumping about. It was warm and weird in a bad way. She shut her eyes tight before she went into the water.

As the evening turned dark, stars appeared in the sky above where Mary Moore floated. She could not see them but they were there. It was so quiet, the water so still. From where I stood, she was like a vision; an angel.

I didn't linger.

TOWNIE

TOWNIE

TOWNIE

THEY TAKE YOU TO TOWN on a field trip. It's Grade 5 and you have a hundred dollars in a white leather purse that belongs to your mother and that you keep strung on your shoulder and held to your hip at all times, like she said.

The bus goes bumping over the highway, knocking you against the window. You cling to the soft ripped material of the cushioned seats. Tears in the fabric are held together with grey duct tape that leaves a dirty black residue where it curls at the corners. And as you cling there, it's an hour drive, you wonder how it happened, the material ripped jagged, like from a knife. The sticky stuff is glue, latching to your fingers but you keep poking at it until the residue is gone and you peel back the tape to get more and by the time you hit the Goulds, the rip is open and fuming a plastic odor tinged with hockey sweat.

Your mother loaned you the purse, and the little change purse inside that closes with a click and holds five crisp twenty-dollar bills. The most money you've ever seen in your life. You hold the purse tight while the bus rollicks and rolls over the southern-shore highway and you sing with the others, the wheels on the bus go round and round, round and round, round and round.

• • •

You are lost on campus, in the tunnels.

Which way, you ask, and they roll their eyes and some girl says it is like a hospital, follow this line or that line depending on where you want to go, blue or yellow or red, but you don't know hospitals either. Some of the hallways have ceilings that hang low like in basements and despite the steady traffic you are certain you will come up against some shadowy figure with a knife in the short jaunt between Sociology 1000 and Philosophy 1200. Even when it doesn't happen again and again, you think of it lurking, leaning in under the pipes.

After class, you meet Ted for coffee to discuss the fifth course. He says there's still time to register. He's in fourth year, so he knows these things. You say double-double because you're not sure and it's what everybody says. The café is alive with thinkers and talkers and people with big headphones, people who know bus schedules by heart and shortcut trails to the mall.

Mom said to give you this, Ted says and hands you an envelope. Your name is written across the front in beautiful looping waves. But you are Beth now. Elizabeth is for old ladies. You screamed this as a teenager from the top of the stairs outside of your bedroom and your mother said that it is a good name, your grandmother's.

You are Beth, and you shove the envelope with the

cheque deep into the pocket of your jeans where it's secret.

What about math? Ted asks.

I hate math.

It's not about liking it. This isn't high school.

I know.

You'll have to do it eventually.

Ted is studying you. You keep your eyes to the table, to the registration booklet. You run your fingers down and settle on Gaelic.

Gaelic, you say. How hard can that be?

• • •

They take you off the bus in a line; leave your stuff. You take the little change purse and shove it up your sleeve and then you have to hold it there the whole time so you won't be found out. The tour is at a recycling facility where they tear Pepsi bottles into tiny squares of plastic like confetti and then they get it down into something even smaller, into sand or something—you stop listening at this part because Jordan Crane snaps Katie Murphy's bra strap and you can't stop giggling. You want a bra, but you don't know how to ask and so you don't and your nipples are getting wider and softer by the day and you can see them through every shirt you own.

The man holds up a test tube and the top is a cap from a Pepsi bottle.

This is how a plastic bottle starts, he says, and he hands them out to you and invites you to take some Pepsi confetti and this is the best part and takes a half an hour and when you are corralled back onto the bus you've managed away with three full test tubes, two for you and one for your best friend, who's in the other class and couldn't come.

Take your seats, Miss says, and you are relieved to find your mother's white leather purse sitting on the seat where you left it and to slide the hard plastic change purse down from the crook of your elbow and place it, with the Pepsi tubes, in the soft silk pockets, zip it up.

The bus ambles away from the depot toward the next tour. It's still morning and all around the pot-holed driveway the bottles are piled in sugary mountains and the seagulls circle and dip, bawling like cats.

• • •

Every Thursday night is cheap student night. The girls in the dorm are drying hair, straightening hair, curling hair. Your roommate, Amanda, shows you the thong she bought at La Senza.

What's that, you ask, and the girls laugh and go back to their mirrors.

La Senza! you say to clarify and they laugh harder and one of them hands you some blush and you dust it all over your face so you look like a whore, they tell you, and then you are sent to the bathroom to wash it off and Amanda does your makeup and marvels at your childishness.

I'm second year, the guy says.

You suck back the screwdriver. There's hardly a hint of vodka.

Business, he says, and you nod. You can't keep your eyes off the sharp hairs that bridge his eyebrows. A babysitter once told you to never trust a man whose eyebrows meet in the middle. He brings you another screwdriver and this time the vodka is strong, like rubbing alcohol.

There is a band. Five guys with long hair and leather jackets and boots with steal toes for kicking things. They're a unit. Practiced. They're writing their own stuff and bobbing their heads like Metallica, but the music is more rhythmic, more rock 'n' roll. You and Amanda and Evelyn dance on the empty floor and they watch and the crowd watches them, watches you, and you suck back another few screwdrivers and then you find Business Major and you drag him to a corridor that leads to a bathroom and he puts his hands up your shirt right away and that ruins the whole thing. You leave him there looking confused and you toss your hair and laugh back at him, and you think that maybe being a townie isn't so bad after all. And when the band leaves the stage, they know a guy at your table and the red-faced guitarist, Jeff, slips an arm around your waist, though you've never met, and you go out with him for two years after that.

• • •

C'mon, Miss says, and you shake your head no. Billy Walsh was laughing at you but now he just thinks you're a pain in the arse and goes on with the others as hot tears run down your face.

Elizabeth, we can't leave you here while we go inside.

I'm not going.

But this is part of the trip.

You shake your head no. The other Miss has gone inside and it's just you and Miss Emberley out here now, and you don't really know why, but you're not going in there.

You like chicken, don't you?

You nod but the tears are running faster now, sobs rising in your throat.

It won't be that bad, she says, and she grabs your hand and tries to pull you to the door, and the sobs escape, tiny strangled things and your eyes are shut fast, your hand tight in hers, pulling her back, slipping back, your fingers white where the blood has leached in her grip.

Don't you want to see how chicken nuggets are made? Miss Emberley says, and you can tell she is getting mad.

I want to see how chicken nuggets are made, she says as you hold rigid at the bottom of the step, and then, Jesus, Beth. It's not like they're torturing animals in there. It's no different than the fish plant, she says.

And then she pulls a tissue from her purse and wipes the snot from your nose and she puts her arms around you and hugs you but you keep your arms in at your sides.

The other Miss is back now, asking whether you're coming, the tour is beginning. Miss Emberley looks disappointed when the heavy steel door shuts and leaves you two out there in the oily parking lot with the bus and the bus driver. She smokes cigarettes while you play with the Pepsi confetti and tell her about all the things you're going to buy at the mall.

When the other kids come out, they are green, except for a few of the boys who are violent with the death of chickens and insist on talking about it, loudly and near you, for the rest of the trip.

• • •

You have a damage deposit that is half your rent and you wonder if you ever get that back.

No, your mother says, and she asks if you have enough groceries. You're still eating the turkey from Christmas. Turkey soup. Hot turkey sandwiches. Turkey, dressing, and gravy wraps. Turkey-lurkey.

You can't imagine moving. This is the best time. This is an apartment with Amanda and her brother and no curfew. Jeff comes over and spends the night whenever you want and he plays his guitar loudly in your room and you shower together and you wake up together and he goes and gets Tim Hortons and you drink your double-doubles in bed between long exploratory sex sessions and first-year readings of Descartes and Hume. You think, therefore you are.

Do you have enough for your bus pass?

Yes.

Are you staying away from the boys?

Yes, you say, and you think of Jeff and you are going to call him as soon as you get her off the phone.

Are you coming home for the weekend?

No.

Your father is buzzing around in the background, wondering his own things. It takes forty minutes to get through it all. They have unlimited long distance.

Twice a month you wait at the apartment on Saturday afternoons for the care package with the Kraft Dinner and spaghetti and bakeapple jam and homemade bread, and your mother puts weird things in there that your roommates don't like, sardines in some sort of mustard sauce, a bottle of mussels. If you are alone when your uncle drops it off, you hide that stuff in your room. One night you eat the mussels with a fork while you study psychology and you are sick for three days and miss an exam. Your doctor's note says food poisoning—unavoidable.

You decide to become a vegetarian but that you will still eat fish, except for mussels. And when you tell your mother, she says what has the world come to.

• • •

They strap you into a seat with Josie Doran and Lucy Worthman, and you are tossed up and about and your neck snaps with the back and forth and you clutch the purse to your side and feel the McDonald's rising in your throat and when it's over you are ejected onto a sunny sidewalk where you spin, dizzy, for a bit and then you go back for more tokens and you line up again.

You've eaten two reams of cotton candy and a box of Junior Mints. You've peed four times and spent twenty-three dollars and seventy-five cents on rides and food so far. At the mall, you buy three CDs and a T-shirt with a Newfoundland flag and chips and candy for the drive home and a black satin necklace that you put your initials on like the other girls and this shared jewelry will bond you for the rest of the school year, set you apart from the girls in the other class who didn't get to go to town.

You are counting for the recounting later. You will write all of this in the small diary you hide between the mattresses of your bed, but not anything bad because your mother reads the diary, even if she says she doesn't.

On the way back, the bus is dark and the country is

thick of fog. It takes an extra half an hour, slow going, and nobody speaks much, your voices strained from screaming and giggling, ooh-ing and ahh-ing. You watch the dim reflection of the roadside markers in the headlights and you drift off with your head pressed to the cool glass. When Miss shakes you awake, there is a dent in your forehead, stretched and red.

· · ·

When summer comes, you have As and Bs, good academic standing. You party goodbyes and pack up your things and head home to wait out the next student loan. You get on a summer project, cleaning garbage and whacking weeds with the high-school kids. You make your room up with posters from the gigs of the new rock stars: the local bands, Jeff's band. Jeff has a car and a summer job at Country Ribbon. He'll come get you on the weekends and you'll go to town to see a show and you'll get drunk and fuck on his sister's couch while she sleeps in the next room, and in August you'll find a place with him and he'll introduce you to people and teach you how to make a barre chord and how to give a proper blow job.

THE SQUARE

THE SQUARE

THE SQUARE

I WASN'T FINISHED TALKING AND I knew the answer. Things moved around us like before. People ate dinner at the café across the street. The sun had ducked below the trees and the streetlamps blinked weakly and I took a long deep breath and held fast my courage and I said it. I had expected to be more nervous. Anyway, there it was, out there, and what a relief.

I'd thought about it for a long while, lying in bed and watching the ceiling, watching the TV but not really watching. I thought about it as I worked and as I drove home in the evenings. It made me nervous to know one way or the other. But here I was. The pigeons hurried on the cobblestones, chasing breadcrumbs. The wind poked at my hair. My clothes felt restrictive. Maybe it was because I knew the word that was coming. I had already wondered how it would sound. Maybe fast and sharp and sure. Or low and scratchy, full of guilt. A choked sound like I'm sorry, just shorter.

I was conscious of the arm near mine, of the body in

the wool coat and gloves. I was conscious of the stiffening of that body as the words escaped my mouth. As I spoke, something changed. Something just perceptible in the energy of our space. I kept my eyes on the square, on the old women who came to feed the birds.

Yes. As soon as I'd finished the last word, I knew. It was in their eyes. They turned too slow in my direction. I was certain. Still, a moment passed before the answer, hung there like water, and I let myself imagine. I entertained the chance that I was wrong. My dreams flew forward. Not a no, but a yes. A yes with enthusiasm. All my hope stood at attention. My doubt was suspended, just for a breath.

Then my ear caught their inhale, and I knew they were about to speak.

I bit the nail on my thumb and then the one on my right index finger.

A man on a bicycle came riding through the square, scattering the birds, so when the mouth formed the word and breathed the word, it was muffled by the cawing creatures and the rubber tires. It was no time for mind reading. I had to be sure.

I turned my head. Met their eyes. I said, sorry, but could you repeat that.

No, they said.

And the pigeons were gone and the streetlamps stretched to full power. The old women went off to prepare suppers and the word, though small, though only a single syllable, echoed out across the square, hopped along the buildings and leapt stellar into the night.

THE CREATION OF WATER

THE CREATION OF WATER

THERE'S A GAZEBO IN THE back where we keep our idols. It stands crumbling against the desert and its wind and storms, open to the elements, its bricks so large and heavy that no man could lift them even with the mechanisms used for such building. My grandfather tells me this when I am young and I do not forget it. It stays with me on each visit I make to touch the tarnished cross, to glance on the pages of the book that falls apart.

What is it? I ask my mother, pointing to it on my last look, the day we travel.

It is God, she says.

But I don't know about that. I see the water rising from the depths of silt, pummeling a wall. The tarnished cross floats across the desert.

• • •

Junot, Mother is yelling, come and put on your apron.

It is the fourth of July and, despite this, I am angry that

I have been given a boy's name. I want her to say June like the rest of the Americans, but she refuses or else forgets and laughs if I make a big deal. In the kitchen, the women are making stews for the party. My grandfather is off buying meat. There is a steak on his list for me. We've been here three months.

Let's be fat, he said, patting his belly, which I know is really made of beer.

Okay, Papa, I said, but he took my uncles and my brothers and is gone for hours, leaving me and my sister with the women to cook.

Peel the turnips, Junot. Bring them here.

They are bulky and there are many to be carried to the little table in the corner. I know Mama wants to show me off. I am the youngest and so, her favourite. I try to smile and be polite. The peeler is small, its handle a miniature cob of yellow corn. At home, colour was everywhere but here it is for holidays and peelers only. It is one of the things we left behind: that and my father, who is dead and so we had to. I am happy to help but in my enthusiasm I shave a thin slice of skin from a finger so that tiny dots of blood appear. I stand there watching them bubble and the women notice. Wash it off, my mother says.

Tapping its beak on the window by the sink is a small brown bird. It looks at me and pecks the glass as if to say let me in. It does not see that the doors all through the house are open. It is free to enter. I try to tell it, motioning with my arms, to go around this way or that. I poke my head outside to show it how and my sudden closeness startles it. It swoops low to the ground and then up to the sky and is gone.

In the back, there is just dust where a yard should be inside a tall fence with chipped green paint. In the middle are the chairs my uncles and grandfather brought over from the community centre, twenty of them spread out in groups that face the stainless-steel barbeque. It shines like a beacon, a lighthouse light. I bet you can see it from space.

When the potatoes are cleaned I help the old lady, Theresa, wrap them in tinfoil and poke holes to let the heat out. I walk them to the barbeque, to Grandfather, and he lays them in first. He says to hold my horses, that it will take hours. The men drink from small cans that they crush on their legs when they are done and toss across the yard, making more beacons, but soon you cannot see them for the feet that dance. The songs from the radio are tinny and distant. They surf the waves of oppressive heat, fold into the colourful skirts of the women.

For a moment, I feel like I'm home. We are dancing outside like it's okay here, too. If I'm not mistaken, though, the real world is below. We are in a dome of chemicals, inhalants. These things we need to keep us breathing. If you break the film of the earth with a needle, our lungs will implode. We will run around with our hands to our necks, the universal sign for choking, knocking into one another, exasperated and blue.

Beneath the sea, my grandfather says, are other worlds. Beneath that tree on the island, there is a city, corrupt and wasting. Birds fly, shrieking, doomed, and they do not know of us. They do not know that their sky is our sea, that there is breath yet, that there is escape. It is only the dark things that know the way to the surface, he says. For in darkness comes an understanding.

It is the desperate who dream most clearly. That, he says, is what Lovecraft meant with Cthulhu.

• • •

I heave the cupboard halfway up the steps, when two men who recognize me from the store offer to help. In your state, they laugh, and shake their heads. They leave full of tea and Mama's cookies and I promise I'll drop in to visit from time to time, after the baby comes. I close the window to keep out the smell of the fish-and-chips shop on the hill, say a little prayer that Bobby will surprise me after work, but I know there's no money. Newfoundlanders are poor like in our neighbourhood. They put bread and spice over their fries and drench the whole thing in gravy, which is just animal fat that is a dull brown and packed with salt. I can't stop eating it.

When Bobby is done, he will be a doctor here in Canada and maybe we will move again, but my mother will come visit sometimes. In California, she has sun and warm wind. Here, on this rocky island in the crass North Atlantic, the days are dark and the streets are heavy with wet snow that mulches black from boots and cars, but there is beauty, too. Church bells ring on Sundays. People say hello on the sidewalk, as if they've met you before.

I push the cupboard into the wall beside the fridge, and drag the radio over so I can listen while I'm cooking. I lay the plastic statue of the Virgin on it, so she can watch over us. Me, Bobby, and our child.

How do you know it is a girl? I ask him when his hand is on my belly, which is most of the time.

I just know, he says. How is it that you don't?

My mother calls and asks how are my feet, did I take my vitamins. Below on the sidewalk, a pair of buskers are setting up, tuning their instruments.

Yes, Mother, I did. Don't worry about it.

What is that noise, she asks.

They're singing, I tell her.

On the street?

On the street, I tell her, and I hold the phone out the window so she can hear them, and so I can hear her smile.

• • •

My grandfather and I are walking behind the house, toward the little gazebo, the room where we said our prayers. Time will not take this place.

Don't they say *ashes to ashes*?

Not this, he says. These walls will fall in waves of water.

The first fish came out of the water and walked on land, he says, did you know that?

I shake my head. I'm not a little girl anymore, I say, and then I look down and I am round and pregnant and a great pain tightens across my belly, doubling me over.

Grandfather enters the gazebo. I waddle behind, my hand at the small of my back, my teeth tight and pressing. Above me, the sky shakes, threatening to split open the shell of our world, revealing another. No, I think. Stay here, I think. Stay here.

Something mighty puts its hands on the shell, on the chemical layer, and pushes. Its thumbs press into the blue horizon, the grooves in its prints big as thunderbolts, black against the clear blue sky, scattering clouds.

Do you believe in evolution, Papa?

When I get next to him, he is standing with the holy book in his hand, turning over a page. It disappears. For a moment he is sad. Then the sunlight peeks through the bricks and he looks up and he smiles and he says, I believe in water.

I wake and the bed is wet and Bobby is running across the apartment, calling a cab. It's okay, you stay there, he is shouting.

I lie back, grip the sheets when the pain hits. Eyes closed, I can feel the heat of home, smell the desert. I see the wall of our gazebo fall, turn to water.

Don't worry, Grandfather says. We took it with us.

And it's true. There is just sand now, not even the impression of a building.

C'mon, Bobby says, the cab is here. He pulls me to my feet. The water runs down my legs in long drips and the baby turns, beating its fists to get out.

Across the desert steps my grandfather. I sing out Papa and he does not turn. He is meeting a man and that man is my father and he's as handsome as I remember him, in black with silver on his belt and the tips of his boots. They start to dance out there, on the horizon, a slow one-two, one-two with hands on hips, one they taught me when I was little.

At the hospital they take my information.

June Marquez, Bobby tells them.

Junot, I say, but they do not hear me.

HOME AGAIN
WITH THE FIRE OUT

HOME AGAIN WITH THE FIRE OUT

TAKE THIS, GERRY SAYS AND he hands me a caplin impaled on three prongs. I hold it to the fire. The skin lifts and crisps, manoeuvers against the heat, then the whole thing slips and lands in the flame, wraps itself onto a log. I haul it out by piercing it. I eat it anyway, because it was caught when the sun was over the water, on the first real roll. Just think, dying to lay eggs like that.

On the beach there are fifteen fires, fifteen tribes. We stoke flames in semi-circles, roasting fish and marshmallows, hoisting brown beer bottles. We want the best fire. The next one over has a perfect steeple built from lengths of 2x4. Rich sacrifices the chairs we'd made from cardboard and duct tape and we step back from the wall of heat. Jenny says how lucky we are to have caught the weather and the last hurrah at the Cobblestone.

A ship blinks across the horizon. I think the ocean is some great beast, that any moment it will rise and climb the beach for us. That it will sound some call we know and all of us, all fifteen tribes, will leave our little worlds of fire and follow it to sea, our marshmallows unmanned and burning to hard plastic black. I wait for it. I think if only that sound, but it is just the rush of the waves sweeping pebbles, the electric shock of the spitting orange night.

I whisper to Gerry, take me dancing.

• • •

It's a thirty-dollar cab ride from Middle Cove, split four ways and the Cobblestone is like a yard sale. There are price tags on the pint glasses, on the flags that line the ceiling, the brass bell and its frayed rope chord. The owner stands out front in his Friday best, announcing the end. We take turns with our condolences and the girl on the door says we smell like fire. The trio plays jazz about the food fishery. The bass struts in salted tones, chasing wayward cod.

There's a table and the cooler is broken so it's what's on tap. We start on the Guinness. Gerry makes a call up the shore and tells them that we've landed. That we're home. He struts back to the table half teary-eyed.

This place back in the day, Gerry says, hand to chest. Let's move back, he says.

C'mon, b'y. You're drunk.

Why not? he says, but he knows why not. He sips his beer and looks away.

We hoist our glasses. Tomorrow this place will be a gourmet hot-dog parlour with foie gras and endive for toppings.

• • •

In the lineup for hangover coffee, we see the Cobblestone owner. He is different in daylight, almost like a normal man. He says that place, how it ran him for so many years. It was his thing, though. The meeting of people. He likes the things that bring people together. Like how we all find ourselves here in this moment, in this coffee shop so far from downtown. Like maybe we're all part of the same thing.

Like a tribe, I say.

He says without the bar he might go into real estate. His friend is an agent, could show him the ropes.

Happy travels, he says.

Up the shore, the gas-stops only sell instant. I get us a couple cups and smoke a cigarette looking out over the water, breathing in the trees. It's a two-hour drive toward she looks lovely, doesn't she, not a day over fifty. The whole town crowds the funeral parlour wondering what are we doing out west, how long are we home for.

We stay up late playing cards with Gerry's parents. I go out to smoke, and check in with the dog sitter. Bo-bo is fine, has had his walkie. Two more days, I tell her, and hang up. Out here it's quiet, except for the sea. From where I stand, I hear it roar and smack the breakwater, demanding entry.

• • •

Out on Water Street, the smokers stand in circles. The talk rises to a din so that nothing is discernible. It's so loud it's quiet again but it's a comfortable beat. Gerry gesticulates, telling a joke. Rich taps Jenny on the shoulder, presents her with a blue flower. Jenny says don't go and she hugs me too tightly. A band of street kids with banjos and accordions swamp a guy into a corner, playing him tunes. I already see these moments as part of some past memory. I've stored them for later. The street kids bow and curtsey and disappear with their instruments into the night, all shadows and tattoos and dreadlocks. The full rose moon sits on the hill, takes their names.

At midnight, the bartender is swamped and sweating in his pint-glass fort. We put $20 in the jar with the toonies and loonies and we head to the park on the harbour front. Rich passes a joint. We say let's hunt the bubble but we can't get close, there's a fence. We're not supposed to be here now. We take pictures from some other wharf, our eyes on the spot where the gulls circle and dive.

Fog grips Signal Hill, runs down in tendrils. It's Portuguese man o' war fog, drawn in the colour of city lights. Rich sings the "Ode to Newfoundland" and Jenny salutes by hiking her skirt up. Rich says she's a tart and she shoves the blue flower into his mouth. We make our way to George Street. Two bars pipe two versions of "Northwest Passage" through overhead speakers. We trace one warm line to the hotdog cart. In the morning, I host a headache of a thousand ice picks.

• • •

135 whales off the point are dancing in caplin. A guy says this like he's counted them. Jenny and Rich drive up to meet us and we eat brie and mussels tinned in brine on crackers that cost $12 a pack. Closer inland, a pair of

humpbacks are chased by a tour boat. On the deck, the tour guides sing Irish songs through megaphones. The music stops the whales from fleeing, it draws them back to circle the boat. They applaud with slapping fins, toss salt ocean at the tourists.

Down the road, the house where I grew up is sunk in with ivy. Rich photographs us walking through the ruins. He says was this your tree and was this your hill and I say yes, that it was all mine once.

At the airport, there's the feeling that you've left something behind. A cellphone charger, a book. Gerry's got his suitcase open on a blue plastic chair. The local paper has a picture of the bar from midnight, of the owner in his suit unplugging the Cobblestone's yellow sign. The caption reads "End of An Era."

Rich asks when are we moving back and Jenny says she's sorry to see us go, she'll miss us again.

The captain says look out over the left wing. In the water, there are whales, hundreds of them, heading for Newfoundland, heading to feed. Gerry leans into my shoulder.

They would never hear us singing this far up, I say, but he's asleep already. He doesn't wake again until we're over the prairies.

SEND MORE TOURISTS, THE LAST ONES WERE DELICIOUS

SEND MORE TOURISTS, THE LAST ONES WERE DELICIOUS

DRIVING'S LIKE DREAMING IF YOU turn off the radio. Your mind has time to loosen, roll itself out flat. Out on the highway there are no dodging dogs, no traffic lights. You can move across the land undetected: notion of person, hint of car. One small movement, though, this way or that, can send you flying at a guardrail, punch your clock.

I keep this in mind on the first winter drive. It's a weekday and there are snow tires at John's and he says come on out.

Where I was raised the rock is grey like steel but here the pavement is strips of cardinal red and dull green like sun-leached seaweed. With its white lines and its yellow lines, the highway is a flag, waving earth.

• • •

How far are we?
Probably about an hour outside.

Outside of what?

What?

Outside of what? Where are we?

I offer him a cigarette and he purses his mouth to receive it. He never takes his eyes from the road, not for an instant. You can't turn the music too loud or he'll shut it off. He says I can't look at that, I'm driving. He says you're not a driver, so you can't know these things.

Gander, he says out the side of his mouth. We're just outside of Gander.

I nod and I try to light the cigarette. He's watching the road and watching the flame that bounces just near his vision and he starts to shake his head, puts his hand out for the lighter. I take the cigarette and light it myself, hand it back. I turn off the air conditioner and roll down the window.

The map has circled destinations and lines. It's looking worn already, bent and folded, the way maps are supposed to look. This is my job: open and close map, light cigarette, pass bottle of water, change CD. St. John's is some distant dream where we rolled out of a parking lot, my father against a screen door crying, his face obscured by the rain. Our last goodbye, 11:42 a.m. Now it is sunny and dry and May 24th weekend and the road is strung with campers and Goldwings. We hit a stretch of highway that is rock wall under wild, green forest. Streams of water slice the rock, the sun makes shadows. The man on the side of the road is waving his arms up over his head, back and forth like an Indy 500 flagman. When we pull up, we see the trouble fifteen feet down a gravel embankment, a car upside down in the bog, its wheels spinning. I think, there are people in that car.

Nick and the man slide down the gravel on the heels of their shoes, their hands cutting on glass and rock. 9-1-1 does not connect immediately. 9-1-1 says who are you and won't listen to the rest and more cars pull up, cars with children and teenagers and one with a surgeon who runs down to help Nick and the man with the first wounded, an elderly woman, who was out of the car, they said. Somehow she got out.

Does anybody have water, and we do, a whole case. A first-aid kit, too, and shock blankets. The woman sits in the front seat and I try to talk to her when they go back for her husband. He is dangling upside down in the driver's seat, they say, but talking. He is stuck in the seat belt.

Hi, I say. It's going to be okay, I say. I tip water to her mouth where the skin is dry from gravel dust. It's like she's been eating it. She drinks a little, then shakes her head away, then drinks a little more. It dribbles down her chin. I say I'm sorry it's not cold. I pull the foil blanket across her shoulders. I get one of the big wooly blankets, too, and I fix her up in that. I sit in the back and people come by and ask how she is and they look at her and they look away. She stares out over the hood like we're going somewhere, like she might say are we there yet, like her husband isn't dangling in a car, like they didn't just go off a fifteen foot embankment at all but this is some other sunny day, some normal day, not a moose to be seen.

Soon the man is walking up the embankment, supported by Nick and the surgeon. They put him in the back seat and he bleeds all over the place. I will find the first-aid kit later covered in blood, all the good bandages used. The surgeon is patching him with butterflies. What is your name? They are from the States. He doesn't know, maybe he fell asleep. How is she doing? he asks, and he puts a hand on her shoulder, says *Josephine,* and she doesn't turn back. She is watching the road ahead, the campers that pull away now the wait is over. A little school of emergency vehicles is blaring towards us.

The EMTs pull everything from the car. CDs crack on the pavement, water bottles go plopping out and across and over the edge of the embankment. The man is walking. The woman is not responding. She's in shock, they say, and they are calling orders ahead to a hospital.

The surgeon shakes our hands and he is gone and the EMTs are gone flashing and ringing with the man and the woman. The wheels on the upturned car stop spinning.

We clean the mess, repack the bottles, clean the stains. It's like we've never been there. By the time we reach the turnoff for the giant squid, we're tired and shaking. We stop at a gas station and smoke cigarettes on a picnic table by the parking lot. Nick hoses off his shoes. Blood and bog runs in rivers through the gravel.

• • •

I reach John's and he is waiting there with boys who are gathered under the hood of a truck, drinking beer from bottles. He looks at my tires and shakes his head. I tell him about her burning gas and he lists off all the things that could be wrong.

The boys have names I can't remember. They are talking transmission. They say hello and then they are silent until I am in the house.

There are hundreds of cars, maybe thousands. They are stacked, backed into corners. Rotting, broken, windshields smashed, bumpers missing. The boys scoot off on ATVs to find new wipers, to find four rims that match. They nod at what's under the hood like it's what they expected. I pour some tea and take a seat at the kitchen table.

• • •

Leaving Montreal, we have stopped talking after the fight. We are two in a car among a hundred other cars, weaving figure eights. When Nick misses the ramp, I say nothing. I have a vision of a shrine. Besides, I'm not supposed to know the way. The air between us is tinder.

Out in the small villages, far from the towers and the traffic and the Saint Huberts, I can breathe. Out here it is expanses of grass and whitewashed houses, little villages that pass slowly. After a while, I try it. I say, you've missed the turnoff. I go back to the window. I roll it down to break the tension. He says put it back up or else turn off the air conditioning. He says there is no point to both.

We pass a sign that says Saint-Anne-de-Beaupre and then he knows. He turns into a parking lot of tourist buses and we get out and smoke on opposite sides of the car. We walk up to the grounds through a small tunnel and sit at an outdoor café at the foot of the lawn of the great church. We drink warm beer under umbrellas that say Coca Cola and Molson Canadian.

Inside is St. Anne, her mummified arm in a glass tube. She was a healer. People leave crutches and wheelchairs near the doorway, walk out on new legs. A crowd of tourists circle the alter, posing for photographs. The arm is on a wall in a case behind a red velvet rope. It doesn't look like an arm. It's some small thing wrapped and disintegrating, part bone and part cloth. It's weird that somebody has cut pieces of a saint's body, sent it halfway across the world to be paraded around. I guess only some parts are acceptable, arms and hands, and feet. The parts used for walking, gesticulating. Probably you wouldn't come across the breast of a saint or a butt cheek or a clavicle. Nothing obscene like that. You'd have to explain what a clavicle was and it would ruin the whole experience and gross people out. Arm is understood. Hand is understood.

Nick has been teaching me the names of bones. He taps on my knee cap and says patella. He taps on my thigh and says femur. He does this sometimes in the kitchen when we are making supper. We stand there looking at the arm they call a relic. He could be a stranger after five years of marriage. He slips off and makes his way down the rows of pews, looking at sculptures, monitoring tourists. Other things here are held behind red velvet ropes, embossed in gold. The light is yellow with treasure. Nick is at the door signaling he's done.

The gift shop has postcards and bottles of holy oil and plastic prayer beads blessed for the tourists. We find gifts for his nan and for my mother, who would never believe me in such a place, and when we get home, I take them to her, a little white statue and a bottle of holy oil, some beads, and she says she has some already, that she saw the relic too. They carried it down from Quebec on a tour to churches and seniors' homes. My mother touched its glass case. She is healed, maybe.

She takes the statue and the bottle of oil. Nick makes us both a cup of tea and pats me on the shoulder. Later he says not to mind her, she's set in her ways. He kisses my hand and holds it all the way back to St. John's. I keep the blessed beads in my pocket. I'm not religious, but you can never been too careful.

• • •

John says she's ready. There are four new tires with square studs for cutting ice and there are new spark plugs. There's some other part, too, that I know is expensive, but they won't tell me how much.

Merry Christmas, he says.

The men wave goodbye from the yard. Twice I get the wrong ramp. I drive for a while in the wrong direction. I think of what they said in driver's training, to relax and to take your time. I stop for a coffee and stand for a while in a gas-station parking lot that's stuffed with trailers and trucks that dwarf my car to dinky. I wish I still smoked so I'd have something to do with my hands.

On Highway 1, the cars go flying at enormous speed. I'm sure above the limit, I'm sure what she can suffer. I toss the coffee cup and head for the right ramp once I see the way, when I am ready.

• • •

The inn has a pub that fits about ten comfortably and everything is wood. There is nothing on tap. I order and I try to finish my work but the waitresses ask what is my name and where am I from and they tell me stories about the town, the guests. I drink three pints and later text back and forth with a woman named Charlene whose boyfriend, Jason, can get me weed, she says, but it doesn't pan out and in the morning I leave to make the ferry.

Across the bridge, the ocean is gone, the seabed an expanse of mud and pools and sometimes what might be a jellyfish. You leave depressions that flood when you lift your shoe. A sign says do not take the rocks, but I fill my pockets anyway. They are conglomerates, fit for jewelry. People have buckets. At any moment, I think the ocean will resist, suddenly and fully, rush in with seaweed and froth to catch us there pillaging.

There is a shack that sells hats with claws and pincers that are supposed to be crabs and have misshapen felt eyes. There are magnets and beach towels and sea monkeys. I buy a mug with a shark that drips blood from white teeth, and text Nick a picture. I make good time back to the highway and fall in line. I am a deserter on a string that's anchored to my island, pulling from my navel, seeking home at 100 km per hour maximum.

It is the Prius's fault but then it's easy to point fingers. It's weaving back and forth, mostly within the lines, like the driver is drunk or texting, mind off elsewhere. I am fourth in a line and three cars pass and it is me and the Prius and a line of traffic behind that pulses with impatience. On the horizon, far off, two tractor trailers mount the hill.

It's now or never, I think, and I signal, pull out into the opposing lane, hit the gas. The Prius swerves dangerously close, then into the shoulder, then at me again. When I get past it, there is relief. I move along the line of cars that are couple with baby and dog, four hippie kids with canoe, guy in SUV, guy in little blue truck. The music gets louder with speed. The open moonroof pulls my hair. It is not until I am passing the little blue truck that I see the trailers up ahead are too close, that it dawns on me that I don't have time. A wave of anxiety hits and then another. Oh shit, I say, then breathe, I say, and I breathe long in through my nose and out through my mouth.

The cars to my right have closed in, are now a line that ripples and stretches, a caterpillar of metal. They separate, they pull in tight, travelling at the same speed. There are four ahead of the truck and there are the two big rigs, coming at me dead on.

A few months back, my driving instructor screamed at me as I hit the highway ramp: faster, faster, go, go, go. I think of how it felt to amp up speed for the first time, to know there was no going back. The only way out, they say, is through. I take another deep breath and I hit the gas.

I creep past two of the cars. As they see me, they start to brake, to slow. They know my predicament instantly. They are alarmed, all eyes. I creep along the third car and the driver is yelling as if I cannot see. I see, I am nodding to show him. I see.

At the head of the line is a rusted red Toyota. 150 brings me to the back door handle and the pedal is tensing near the floor. The form of the first tractor trailer driver is not so far off now. It sits up straighter in its seat.

I reach the driver's door of the red rusted Toyota and the woman turns her head and sees me. She turns her head again, again. She sees what I see, that there is no time. She is looking in the rearview, leaning on her brakes, but the caterpillar is a thing of its own with many legs and parts that will jumble and fall ahead if you're not careful.

The woman looks at me, then looks ahead. She looks a look that says I'm trying.

Thank you, I say. I try to glance this to her, grateful. Breathe, I think. Smile.

She looks at me to say she is trying. This is the best that she can do.

I know this and then I am sorry. She will think of this forever and wonder about me, what was wrong, what was I thinking. Nothing, I would like her to know. Nothing is wrong. Or at least, I didn't mean to do this. I see the bigness of the tractor trailer descending, its grill angry teeth taller than my little rental car. I also see that if I can't get in, I'll have to go off the other side. It's that or a pile up. It's that or everyone will die, not just me. Everyone will be mangled. Baby, dog, hippie canoe crowd, SUV, dude in blue truck, woman in red car.

She looks to say they are slowing and they are slowing, I can feel it but the pedal is on the floor and the move ahead is slow. I've never driven so fast. I am moving ahead and then the woman is gone. In the side mirror, I can see her shock.

The nose of my car passes hers and the trailer is nearly at me. The driver is raising a hand to pull the horn but he puts it back down. He knows I know. He is taking a deep breath. It is just me versus the tractor trailer, coming at speed, this giant of metal and gasoline and god knows what he's carrying and can this car go any faster and I am sure I don't want to drive this fast ever again and can I get ahead and the long line of traffic pulses metal in the sun.

My passenger door passes the Toyota's front bumper. If I move in too quickly, it's over for the woman. It is me and her or me and the tractor trailer or it is me, and I am not god. I am not close to god. And if it's her or me, it's me down over the embankment. This is what death looks like, sudden and at the end of a long trip. The trailer whips closer. We're going to hit.

And this is where time slows. This is where somebody, something, steps in and turns a dial down and everything is slow motion, hair trigger. I see the white paint on the front of the tractor trailer, how it's scratched in places, long drags of black or metal from unfortunate animal horns or other things, like me. I can see the driver's thick hair, the cut neat like a schoolboy's, that it's healthy and brown. His chair is yellow, quilted behind him in the lonely white cab.

I am as fast as I can be.

The air ripples static.

In the side mirror, I see the red rusted car is almost behind me and this is it. Time is a snail, slipping greasily.

I cut the wheel.

The caterpillar shakes and ripples, the red rusted Toyota veers dangerously onto the shoulder. I am at 200 in a small can of tin as the tractor trailer flies past me and the next trailer too, bigger than the first and they are gone, like that, and my wheels are lifting from the highway and okay, I think, don't cry, I think, and tears well up and I slowly begin to lift off the gas.

The caterpillar shrinks back but I am flying. I cannot stop. I say out loud, don't cry, as the speedometer creeps back and time is time again and much too fast, zipping along in a blur, out of control.

It's yellow line, asphalt, yellow line, asphalt and then gravel spins out and she starts to fishtail but slowly I brake and a long time later I stop and I am bawling and the man from the little blue truck is beating on my window yelling did you want to die, did you want to die.

• • •

I pass a smear of crimson, the suggestion of a rabbit. The rocks are brush painted in white. Roxanne loves Billy. Dennis wuz here. The man ahead of me is carrying two Christmas trees on a trailer. I wonder who the other one is for. He went off and cut them. Christmas: death to a million trees. The new studded tires spin percussion with the pavement: vroomp-vroomp, vroomp-vroomp, vroomp-vroomp.

Up ahead, the yellow lights aren't flashing, but there is a moose on the highway. I stop behind the other cars. We are in a line, headlights blazing, and the moose is our leader. We wait for orders but he does not know them yet. He is watching something in the distance. To him, we are not there. We are inconsequential. We shine spotlights on the molting coat and he snorts cold breath into the night.

There is talk in the paper of a cull. Moose are discussed like terrorists, like they have intent. Look how they interfere with our lives, with our highways. The accidents. They're not native. Look how they bound out from the brush, full pace, and are on us, just like that. Look how they stand, immovable. We've erected fences and set up alarms. We've hunted them. The signs get bigger, the antlers on the signs get bigger, and still they come, still they breed.

This guy knows he's a bull. He stomps, kicks up road. Someone yells out a window and he does a little trot, makes a dart like he's going but he doesn't, he stands his ground. He moves in closer, his breath fogs a windshield.

RIDING WITH MAURICE

RIDING WITH MAURICE

YOU NEED TO FIND A way to get out of bed. You know the floor
is there, carpeted. You know the coffee is downstairs in the
cupboard. You just pour it in tablespoons into a filter, dump
in the cups of water, press the button and it will turn red.
These are things you could do when you get up.

The cheque in your account is waning from interest.
The bills are unpaid. What is the point of washing dishes?
They will get dirty again. What is the point of cleaning? Of
shaving? Showering? The body keeps producing hunger,
hair and sweat. Your mother has called three times to ask
you over. Otherwise, nobody has phoned/texted/emailed
in four days. You can count the days: one, two, three, four.
If you make it to six without becoming desperate and
contacting them, you will make a pizza and watch a movie
as a treat. You will do this alone, unless you give in and ask
somebody. You won't ask anybody. If they wanted you, they
would be here now.

The shower is wet and warm, or it will be. There is hot
water in the tank. The walls have a roof that keeps out the

rain, and the rain is teeming.

Work is just there on the computer. Pull it up. Two hours tops. Top dollar. But the bed is an envelope.

Sometimes when things get close, when you have to do things, the body rebels. You feel like a child about to throw a tantrum. When the person picking you up comes, you will flip the hell out.

Get out of here, you will say. Get out of here, Maurice.

You have this urge and so it is painted on your face when Maurice pulls up and the horn beeps shrill and, because he doesn't come in, you have the moment where you are putting on your shoes to calm down. Think of your next move. You are sick, you could say, or tired, but this is the only day he can drive you to the grocery store and you have nothing in the fridge but a near-empty crusted mustard bottle and two slices of bread. It's like being a student, but it's self-inflicted. An education in last resorts.

How are things?

Same.

Are you taking your pills?

Yeah.

It is like this all the way to Merrymeeting Road. Your shoes are wet from parking-lot puddles, your feet squelch through aisles of cans. Maurice is dating this girl and here's her picture. If you buy ten boxes of Kraft Dinner and two cartons of milk and a tub of butter, you can eat all week without surprises and you can just use the microwaveable bowl. You can throw the dishes out with the trash and then you don't have to wash them. Maurice wants to marry this girl, he says. He wants you to meet her. You give him a look. You can buy new dishes at the thrift store in a few weeks if you need them.

$25.40, the checkout kid says and Maurice says are you sure that's all and Maurice says it's on me and he carries the stuff back through the rain to the car and he holds you in the car, in front of the house, and gives you a speech while the water washes over the windows. You step outside and everything is wet and, man, you have to get yourself together.

Kraft Dinner is cheese and milk and butter. It's probably not food, but it's warm and it's easy to eat when propped against pillows. You've watched this movie five times this week but some of it is new still. It's easy to sleep during the familiar parts. When you wake, you turn it on again, somewhere random.

Maybe later you'll work, you think, and you do. Six hours in total.

Maybe later you'll wash the bowl, you think, and then you forget and what difference. Kraft Dinner is Kraft Dinner.

The clock ticks time away. Where does it go, time? Is it a thing at all? You ask your mother when she calls. She says are you okay. She says she can get someone out there.

Maurice calls and says it's Tuesday again. You've had three showers since you saw him last. You say you have no money for groceries. It's a sunny day when he pulls up. He has more info on the girl. He has plans on Friday night. He says come out with us and there is that anxiety.

He says, how are things?

You drag across the parking lot, nodding at more pictures.

You can get a box of chicken nuggets and a value bag of fries and four litres of pop and there's ketchup at home already. Maurice is considering a resort in some hot country. Here is what he says it costs for two people. Frozen pizzas are on sale. Pepperoni and cheese or Canadian. You can only have one. Maurice buys, Maurice drops you off. He says can I come in and you say not fit, b'y, not fit. You drop a can of milk on Queen's Road and you stand and watch it roll into traffic.

You eat the pizza and the cookies. You eat the chicken nuggets. You watch *Silence of the Lambs* four times. You do three hours of work, Clarice. You take one shower. You've mapped the patterns of your thoughts on the walls of your room. There is lonely. There is hope.

Maurice calls to say it's Tuesday.

In the car he says, how are things?

The girl is in the front passenger seat looking at you with big eyes. It's like she wants something from you. She checks her makeup in the side mirror.

The sky looks like rain again. You are craving French fries. You know the store is there, waiting.

Maurice says, are you taking your medication?

THREE MEN
WALK INTO A BANK

THREE MEN WALK INTO A BANK

THREE MEN WALK INTO A bank, but not together.

The First Man

The First Man who walks into the bank is unkempt and wearing a track suit. He is short with greasy hair and a local accent. He fidgets nervously with a cheque and takes his place at the back of the line. Six feet to his left is the shiny black door. Six feet is the average height of the three men.

The person who first notices The First Man is the girl immediately in front of him. It is because he stands too close. She pretends to text.

The First Man's phone rings, everyone looks up. It takes a while for him to answer. He has the conversation they rehearsed.

Hey.

Sorry, I couldn't get to the phone.

How is your leg? Is it swelling?

I have to change a cheque.

Yeah, sure.

He does not say the kill phrase.

The First Man disconnects. Poor bastard, he says. The girl in front looks back, looks away.

The Second Man

The Second Man stands at the automatic teller in the porch. He carries a bankcard with the information of an alias, someone who does not exist. He exists. He is tall and handsome and his clothes are perfect and fitting as if stitched for him, which in fact they were. A button-up shirt and blue jeans with store creases. There are to be no mistakes, Miguel had said.

He slides the thin plastic card into the automatic teller. He punches in the PIN. It spells 2587, which spells B-L-U-R. The Second Man is not good with codes or with numbers. He is a man with the type of calm who can stand at the ATM and use only the body language necessary to communicate to The Third Man that the alarms are disabled and The First Man is approaching the teller. There are to be no unknowns.

He pulls out forty dollars and turns as if to leave, stuffing the two twenties into his wallet as The Third Man, who has read his signals properly, comes through the door.

The Third Man

The Third Man closes his phone, looks to The Second Man for the signal and enters the bank. The Third Man is wearing a blonde suit jacket, a tan shirt and slacks. His hair is frosted. It's so blonde, he looks German. He is blonde at heart, maybe, he thinks. The hair feels good.

He meets the eyes of The Second Man in the porch. He also meets the eyes of a woman waiting in line for the ATM.

The Third Man takes his time as he opens the inner door. He is the signal for The First Man that they are a go.

His walking through the door says that: *go*.

The First Man

Sees The Third Man, and that is his cue. He feels a tightening in his chest. He runs his thumb across the blade in his pocket and the teller says next. He runs it across the teller's throat right after she says and what can I help you with today, sir. There is screaming.

The Second Man

Secures the exits. Ties hostages.

The Third Man

Jumps onto the counter. He yells this is a stickup, like he always kinda wanted to yell. He yells where is the fucking manager? He holds the dead teller's head by the hair and he screams it again, get me the fucking manager.

Sir?

A trembling mass of man stands in a doorway.

You the manager? The Third Man asks, letting the head drop.

Yes, sir.

This man is just about to piss himself.

The Third Man points his gun at the shiny black door.

That, he says. Open it.

The First Man

Is the last one out with the loot. They pull him into the back seat of the car and drive off, tires squealing. There are no sirens, like he expected. The whole thing feels sort of like a tantrum. Like drama for nothing.

They ditch the rented van at a cul-de-sac four blocks up and they scramble into the SUV where Miguel is waiting. Miguel pulls The First Man's face to his, kisses him full on the lips.

Good job, my friends, he says, and claps his hands together. Good job.

The First Man thinks of the teller's head lolling on the counter, the bank manager's brains blown out all over the money in his bag. The colours of the trees are the same, the shadows in the sun are the same, but he is not. He has killed. Miquel says his debt is now paid.

The Second Man

Is driving the car. Is rounding the bend when he comes smack dab into a police barricade. He slows and stops and Miguel says what is this and, for a few moments, the four of them sit there in the car, idling.

The Third Man

Is silent. Is thinking. Is trembling.

The First Man

Says we're done for and Miguel says stop talking, let me think and then don't be foolish and then shut up! But this last part is screamed and spit lands in The First Man's face.

The Second Man

Says oh I don't know we can't get through we can't get through we can't get through fuck and Miguel lays a hand on his shoulder.

The Third Man

Says he has an idea. The Third Man says, hand me the money.

Miguel says, what?

Hand me the money.

No fucking way.

I have an idea.

So what is it?

Do you have an idea? The Third Man asks, and besides, there is no time.

Miguel says do not fail me, brother.

The Third Man steps from the car with the bags of money.

An officer yells from a megaphone, says everyone put the bags down, says everyone exit the car. The Third Man shakes his head no to his companions. As in, do not exit the car. They sit still.

The Third Man lays the bags on the ground and his gun, too. He removes his coat to show the officers he is not armed as he steps slowly towards them. He waves a hand across the air in front of him and a strange film forms, something silvery blue, like it's coming off his glove.

The officer says everyone exit the car immediately and The Third Man rubs the air some more and something is appearing there, something with form, something solid. Miguel smiles.

The First Man

The First Man feels dizzy, like the world turned upside down. He is seeing but he cannot believe it. It defies understanding. The Third Man is wiping out the air in the middle of the street and in its place is a door. Well, the beginnings of a door.

No, that doesn't seem right.

The Third Man is somehow making a door, like magic, in the middle of the air on the street between them and the cops. It's a blue and silvery door but it's a door nonetheless. The First Man clasps his chest.

Miguel is slapping the dashboard and saying bravo, bravo. There is a thin film of air that shivers between where they sit in the car and where the police sit, weapons drawn over bonnets and trunks.

Cars back up down the street and the first drivers get out of their cars to witness. The First Man didn't know doors could be beautiful but now that he knows he trys to think on other beautiful doors and this one, this giant of a door, in its shades and nuances, is by far the most beautiful he has ever seen.

It is so stunning, the spectacle, that when Miguel and The Second Man step from the car and join The Third Man, The First Man keeps his seat.

And it is so jarring to The First Man that when Miguel and the Second and Third Men step inside that door to that other place, The First Man cannot know that he does not notice. That he sees some of the bags of money fall to the ground. That finally, they have left him alone.

He watches the door that rolls itself up into itself, and then is gone, and he is surrounded.

• • •

Where are they?

I don't know.

Where did it lead?

It's been like this for hours, sweating in a tin room. They won't give him cigarettes. He's pissed his pants from the beating, afraid.

Lawyer, he repeats for the millionth time.

Where did it lead?

The voice of the detective ricochets from wall to wall in a thin echo, hard on the ear. She is positively beside herself about the door. They all are.

I don't know, The First Man says again and again. The detective pounds a fist on the table and says this is not good enough.

They've gone over it and over it and The First Man cannot remember. He cannot remember how he met them, where they came from, where they were. He remembers that there was a debt and that it was paid, that there was a door from nothing in the middle of the street.

Did they see it? He is dying to know.

We ask the questions, not you. We ask the questions.

They leave the room. Leave him in there alone. This keeps happening too. The First Man grows tired.

The Second Man

The Second Man is thankful, but he doesn't know what is happening. Somehow he is in here, this new place, with The Third Man and with Miguel. It is a country to which he has not been.

The Third Man and Miguel go off to figure things out and The Second Man is to stay put near the door. It will remain there for a while, a portal, and must be guarded. He's not sure why.

The Third Man

The Third Man tells The Second Man not to let anyone near the door. The streets are black with rainwater and the energy he's expended makes him tired and he slips and grows irritated. This causes Miguel to laugh at him, which angers him more.

Here, Miguel says, and they duck into what looks like a hotel. One last glance onto the square shows The Second Man waiting patiently in the street.

Sir, sir?

Yes, the maître-de asks.

May we have a room.

The First Man

Has been waiting for forty minutes now, but he would swear it has been much longer. He is tired of waiting, tired of all of it.

Fuck you, he says to the girl cop when she comes back again, all angry still and holding a phone.

Call them, she demands.

What?

You have a number in your phone for Miguel. We ran the records. I want you to call them, plan a meeting.

They won't believe me. They know I'm caught.

Tell them you escaped somehow.

I killed somebody, The First Man says, but he doesn't

know why.

Tell them we know where they are and we want to make a deal.

Look, lady, these are some smart fucking guys, okay? They won't buy it.

Do it, she says.

Why don't you do it?

I don't speak arsehole, she says.

The Second Man

Gets a call from Miguel that says he has a room and they will soon be back for him. The Second Man is to wait at the door for a while longer.

The Third Man

The Third Man pours Miguel another drink and sits back on the couch and makes conversation. Miguel goes to the toilet and this is where The Third Man gets him, from behind while he's pissing. He puts his gun to the back of Miguel's head and blows his brains onto the gold-framed picture of rhododendrons that hangs on the wall near the sink. Piss and blood pool around his shoes.

The dutiful Second Man is waiting in the street, like he was told. Like a dog sworn to stay. The Third Man shoots before The Second Man even sees him approaching.

The First Man

Is surprised when The Third Man steps into his cell. The men in the opposite cell are on their feet, watching, when The Third Man steps out of the door. The beautiful blue door makes a sound when you're up close, The First

Man now knows. A kind of humming or buzzing, like it's electric.

The First Man listens to The Third Man, how the other two are dead, how the money is all theirs. The First Man has bruised lungs and a court date and decides fuck The Third Man's plan, and fuck The Second Man and Miguel too. He of course changes his mind when The Third Man mentions the money. The Third Man needs an accomplice. The Third Man says he figured The First Man perfect for the job, mostly because he is stupid, no offence. Don't take that as an insult so much as a plainly stated fact.

The First Man nods. He agrees on account that he didn't do all that good in school. And also, The Third Man is magic.

Fine, he says, and The Third Man and The First Man step through the door and into the police evidence room.

The Third Man
Holds the door.

The First Man
Shoots the guard and takes the keys and helps The Third Man rummage through the new bags until they come across the rest of the money. The First Man takes a big block of cocaine he finds in a drawer. It's marked pure. He takes it because why the fuck not.

The Third Man
And The First Man walk out of the station, the front door. The Third Man says thank you, friend. He sees The First Man has been good, loyal. He doesn't point out that there

are surveillance tapes at the station. The First Man just waves as he walks away, poor fucker.

The Third Man leaves The First Man downtown on a corner with his cut of the money and the block of cocaine. He walks back through the station and through the beautiful blue door in the evidence room, which rolls up neatly behind him and, poof, is gone.

The First Man

Sits looking out over the bay, thinking about doors. How one is supposed to close and another open.

He stands and tries to muster his energy, points his finger to the air, and nothing.

Somewhere in the distance, there are sirens.

IN DREAMS

IN DREAMS

PASS THE KETCHUP, KRISTA SAYS and follows the arm that moves across the counter. Thanks, she says. You're welcome, Jerome says. Todd and Lisa honk the horn. Krista blushes. On the walk home, they fall into the bushes, her hair catching on branches.

Is this okay?

Yes, she says.

This is how James is invented. Krista realizes him in the bushes, is sure of him on the walk home. She considers him at school on Monday. James will be six foot, like Jerome. He will never have sex in the bushes, though, and he will have her chin, her lips. He will recite poetry like the boy in fifth period she has a crush on. He will get a job as an engineer and marry a nice woman named Judy and he will let Krista move in with them when she's old. She knows him already, these things and that he'll love art and good food and that he will be determined.

Yeah, but how do you know? her friend Susan asks. She hands Krista the pregnancy test in the aisle of Power's

Drugs and Krista grins.

It's in his nature, she says. His birth sign.

She has charted it all out during Chemistry and Physics. He will be Taurus. He will be sandy-haired.

At eight he will fall from a bike and cut himself badly. There will be a scar that he will have to explain and this will be how he develops his excellent sense of humour. He will try stand-up twice at the age of twenty at the campus bar and get booed off stage. He will tell jokes to his bosses and his lovers and he will make them laugh, and make Krista laugh too, even if she is having a bad day. He will play soccer.

Krista, it's Jerome again.

Tell him I'm out.

He keeps calling, Krista.

Tell him anyway.

J-A-M-E-S. She writes the letters in cursive on lined exercise paper, thinking of the test, waiting for the alarm to sound. Susan glances nervously at the bathroom door, then jumps when Krista's mother comes with cereal bars and milk.

You should call that boy back.

I will.

James will live to be sixty-three and have two sons. Krista will die when he is forty-three, ovarian cancer. On her death bed he will sing her a song she used to sing to him when he was little. She is choosing it now, standing in the bathroom with Susan. She says wait, and Susan sits on the toilet and claps her hands saying come on, come on, look at it.

"In Dreams" by Roy Orbison.

Krista! Christ's sake.

But just before the dawn.

Look, if you don't look—

I awake to find you gone.

I'm looking, Krista.

I can't help it. I can't help it. If I cry.

It's negative, Susan says. She is holding up the white stick that has one line only.

Krista, it's that boy again.

Hi, Krista says.

Hi, says Jerome.

DEEP BLUE SEA

DEEP BLUE SEA

DEEP BLUE SEA

HE'S SITTING AT A TABLE in the corner. The curtains behind him are drawn, blocking out the view of the street. There's a vase with flowers by his elbow.

You slip him the twenties under the table. His hand fiddles around for yours and hits your knee, your upper thigh, then fumbles over your fingers, gripping the bills and ripping them away in a wad. You feel people watching. And you're not the type to bend money. Legal tender and all that. The bag he puts in your hand is small.

It's good, he says. Uncut.

Thanks, man.

Do you know who I am?

No.

If you get me a beer, I'll tell you a joke.

Sorry, that was all the money I had.

Oh well, he says. Another time, then. And he sweeps an arm out to usher you away. His next customer is in the corner, eying you, waiting for your chair.

On the street, the wind takes your scarf and snaps it

straight. When you pass his window, the curtains are open, the bar lies vast and empty.

• • •

The first one to go is your mother, though you should have seen it coming. She had that cough that went on for years, the one she never got checked, first nor last. You find her lying on the bathroom floor on a Saturday morning, your stomach already reeling from hangover, and the shock of it slides you to your knees and you don't know how long you're there crying, soundless, before you come to and dial 9-1-1.

People bring food after the funeral and say how lovely she looked and where did you find that dress and you smoke some pot with your older brother on the swing set out back.

Are you going to be alright? he asks. You know, out here on your own?

Fine, you say, but you're not sure. The nights are dark out here, the roads foggy. Nobody comes out this way, not even for drives.

One of the aunts is beckoning you inside. She will stuff you full of casserole and tiny ham and cheese sandwiches and chase you off to bed, saying a good night's sleep cures all, but you'll wake at two with a craving and you'll be pulling your boots on and clearing the driveway before the dog lifts his head to note your passing.

• • •

He's not there, but the flowers are, and a small paper box, folded in purple and silver and two tones of blue, that has your name on it.

I am sorry for your loss, the card inside reads.

And underneath the card, another small baggie. Free of charge. And in the corner of the baggie a little white pill that has "Eat Me" written on it.

You take a seat at the bar, pondering the gift as the bartender draws you a pint of Guinness.

Excuse me, you say, but when was he here?

Who? she asks.

The man with the flowers.

I don't know what you're talking about, she says, and when you point to the corner, the flowers are gone.

You chalk it up to grief, and head home to straighten out and try to sleep.

• • •

The officer at your door is young. The cap in his hand is shaking as he delivers the news. Your brother and his wife, such a tragedy, and on their way back from such a tragedy.

I'm sorry, he manages and then bursts into tears. The older constable leads him back to the cruiser and the neighbours are in their windows, wondering on the fuss, and all goes askew in the world, top becomes bottom and bottom top, and your stomach rolls and thunders and your legs go limp. The neighbour ladies have you by the elbows and are carrying you to the couch. You imagine your brother splashed across dull grey pavement and you wonder if he had a moment of awareness, just a split second, when he crashed out like that, before the spirit leaves the earth or whatever happens happened. You can smell the casserole reheating. As the mourners reappear, you make your excuses and head to the room.

You find your mother's cat curled up on the centre of her bed, and you slide in beside it and you think of your mother and your brother and the grief has your head splitting. You go through half the baggie, and it was the last of it anyway, a thought that fills you with panic, starts you rifling through your pockets for the cash your uncle pressed into your hand the day before.

The bar is closed, that much is certain. Even if somebody answered, you couldn't get in. Licenses and all. Regulations. You wonder if he hangs out somewhere else, if you might be able to track him down on George Street someplace. You make a note to ask for his card next time. He seems the type to have a card.

You turn the baggie over in your hands and the little white pill says Eat Me, but you think you've heard wrong, and you think how tired you must be. And you seal it back up in the little baggie and you put it in the top drawer of your dresser on your way back to the living room, where the women sit and chat and knit and watch over the cooking and wonder what will be the end of it all.

• • •

The next evening you stop in on your way from the funeral director, but the table is empty. No flowers, no note. You ask around, but they don't know him, they say, or he could be this guy or that guy. Why don't you try here or there, they say, but outside the aunts are squirming impatiently in the car, and Jeff's college buddies are flying in from Denver, a contingent of them, and Cara's family too, and there are beds and prayers to be made before the night is out, and Uncle William has a heart attack at dinner, which throws everything off altogether.

The cousins and neighbours and mourners, the whole bloody cult of them who've been living in your house for near on a week, go off with William to the hospital.

You're sure you're okay? they ask.

Do you want us to stay?

Would you like some stew?

Can I draw you a bath?

But you shut the door on them and take the stairs two by two and by the time the little pill says Eat, you've swallowed it whole and half a fifth of vodka besides.

• • •

The night rolls on in frightening dreams and everywhere is he, and he is everywhere.

The aunts cry at the locked door of your bedroom, but you cannot raise yourself from the bed where you thrash wildly. You hear your voice screaming. In the dream, your arms rise and fall with waves of fright. The deaths and their details staged over and over in streets and in cars and in rooms, the man ever-present and watching from the table with the flowers, sipping tea.

The aunts have you by the legs, they're holding you down. When you come around, you can still feel the asphalt cutting across your cheek, the loose feeling of bobbing across the pavement, all hands and no sight. You can see it all from where your head lolls on the ground, next to that of your wife.

• • •

They bury your brother and uncle. The aunts have you propped up between them for the standing parts of the ceremony. The neighbours nod as you are shuffled by with a rose for the grave and shuffled back to your seat, but you don't see. You're still with the nightmares. They lie, opaque, over the starched white shirts and black suits of the men and women who have come to see your family off. The air swims like smoke.

• • •

You don't even look when you walk in this time, but he is there. You felt him as you approached. The bartender dries a glass, the same one over and over, and eyes you suspiciously. You walk to his table, take a seat. You reach a hand underneath, looking for his hand, extend the few twenties. He puts the baggie in your hand.

It's good, he says, but you don't answer.

He comes at you from behind as you are doing up your coat and offers you a flower from the vase, a white carnation. When you don't move to take it, he slides it into your breast pocket so it's poking up through the buttonhole.

You are crossing Duckworth when you see you have messages. One from Aunt Mary, another from Aunt Joan, telling you to call, that something's wrong, that something's happened.

You can smell the casserole cooking, hear the knitting of the needles. The car slams into your right side, breaking the rib that punctures your lung and starts the blood in a slow rise to your throat, bubbling onto your tongue, cutting off air. You're hands and knees on the pavement, spitting out teeth, stumbling from one side to the other, reaching for the baggie that got heaved a few feet with the impact. The new pill is yelling Eat Me! And you're afraid you'll be the last to reach it, so you don't stop, despite the pain.

They are telling you to hold still, to wait. They are whimpering at the sight of you, all bloody and foaming at the mouth, out there ruining their sunny afternoon, out there dying on a public street.

You get to it at last, tear open the baggie and shove the pill and the powder into your mouth, but you can't swallow for choking. When your body slows and your head hits the pavement, you're sure you see him walking from the bar, a tall man with an empty vase and a slow smile spreading.

ECRU

ECRU

ECRU

THE PRICES HERE ARE THROUGH the roof, Dave says.

I say that I like the neighbourhood. They've booted out the ruffians—save that one house at the bottom. They've bought things up, torn down rotting walls, poured new foundations. They've rebuilt the street in row-house blue, row-house orange, row-house yellow.

I like the garden out back, and the grapes that grow green and turn purple and hang in perfect bunches from the arbour. I like to sit out there and imagine making wine, even if I don't make it. We'll find the time this winter, I'll say to Dave, and he'll nod as he always nods and then we'll forget again. I want the possibility of wine. I take all of the visitors down to show them.

Imagine, grapes in St. John's, I say.

Imagine, they say, and Dave nods, accommodates. He wants to move to Conception Bay South.

Here there are musicians and artists, drunks, oil workers, a gossip who stands on her front stoop most of the day and has convinced most of downtown she's homeless.

I see her out walking with a backpack and plastic bags full of clothes, asking for change. She pretends she doesn't know me.

So there's no problem, then, Dave says more than asks.

There is, in the red house, the man who beats his wife, and his wife, and at least one cat, a small calico with a bell on its neck. The neighbours on either side are charged with phoning 9-1-1 when things get bad. We've never known her name. We were introduced once and he did all the talking. She just stood there, hands folded at her waist, her face to the ground between walls of auburn hair.

What if it goes too far some night? Dave wants to know. He is clenching and unclenching his fists, cracking his knuckles. What if he kills her and we have to live with that?

We'll have to live with it either way, I tell him. Here or wherever. Death is the kind of thing that follows you around. We should stay here, I say and run my hands along the clapboard. We'll have to paint, of course.

Dave chews his lip and goes back inside. The calico turns slow circles in the window of the house of the man who beats his wife, then curls into a ball and is asleep. From the step, I watch the fog roll up the hill to Cabot Tower, just past the roofs of Livingstone.

• • •

I'm walking down Queen's Road so I stop at the convenience store for cigarettes. The clerk asks my ID, not because he thinks I'm eighteen but because he thinks it's funny with my roots showing. I have to do it because his boss is there, so I rummage through my purse and find my driver's license.

I'm thirty, I say, as I hold it up for him to see and there's that sly grin of his.

He wants to fuck me is what this is all about. One night at the Spur he left his teenaged blonde at a table and came striding up to where I was sitting at the bar.

You're a musician, aren't you? he asked.

No.

What do you want, the bartender asked him.

Her, he said, pointing his finger at me. How much for her?

The bartender handed me an India and took his money. That's a start, she said, and he laughed. Then he noticed the blonde watching him and he straightened a bit.

Girlfriend? I asked.

Wife, he said, and then, it's amazing what women will believe.

He took the change and went back to the table. She looked satisfied with whatever explanation he provided.

In broad daylight, he's not as handsome. In the daylight, his face is pockmarked, his hair is flat and dull and his jeans hang down to his knees, revealing a pair of SpongeBob SquarePants boxer shorts.

You can stop carding me already, I say.

Then what will we talk about, he says.

• • •

Conception Bay South is where Dave's sister lives with her husband and kids. His parents bought the land next to hers, but never built on it.

It could be ours, he says, and he turns the car so the passenger side is pulled up along the lot's expanse, so I can get a good look. He puts his hand on my knee.

We'll have a big yard, he says.

We have one now.

Bigger, even, he says, and leans in. For kids, he says.

The earth here is torn up. Churned. Bits of asphalt from an old driveway are tossed against a few rolls of sod, like someone was here and changed their mind.

It needs grading, Dave says, but it's not bad. We could be moved in by the spring. Judy and Mike next door. We could see our nieces and nephews more often. Go for long walks.

We drop our coats on a chair in the foyer where Judy has hung a banner that says Congratulations in silver block letters and miniature bouquets line the hallway. I grab the back pockets of Dave's jeans. The only suitable dress I could find is hugging too tightly.

Just an hour, he says, and turns to kiss my forehead.

Trays of veggies and chips and dips and pigs in blankets line the dining-room table. The kids are screaming and running so Judy yells at them from time to time, which doesn't slow them down a bit. Dave heads to the patio with the men.

So I hear you're thinking of building out here, Judy says, and a ripple goes through the crowd. Ooh, the women say, and yes, g'rl! They are in unison, the women, pretty much all of the time. There is Dave's sister Judy, his mother Barb, his cousins Lana and Candice, his aunt Minnie.

Oh, it's not for sure, I say and pick at a sliver of red pepper.

Cul-de-sac. Family home. Backing on a greenbelt, for privacy. Draperies and marble countertops and what are you going to paint the living room? Open concept, they've already decided.

Ecru is big, Judy says, and puts her hand to her chest, asking us to linger on the word. The women nod at me and smile.

It's like beige, she says. But different.

You should go with that, Barb says, and handing me a stack of napkins, she pushes me off to the living room. She is regal and proud in mother-in-law ivory. A schoolteacher once, retired young. We got drunk together at the last wedding and she said she didn't exactly hate me, and it was a funny thing to say and made it easier to talk to her after that. At least we both want what's best for Dave.

Barb is familiar with the making of paper swans, the beautifying of rooms. She is fast behind me, tut-tutting and re-doing my work, spreading each napkin, then folding expertly. I manage three to her ten.

It's the style this season, Barb says. Ecru. She laughs. How lucky are we to be worrying about paint and napkins with so much going on in the world.

We return to the kitchen, where the conversation thankfully turns to other things. Heads shake. Wine is poured. Gossip is shared. The children go running by with sticky hands, and have to be scolded away from the stove where the food is cooking.

Dave and the men are laughing when Judy opens the door with their refills. They watch politely as she sets down their drinks and lays out the snacks. She slides the patio door closed slowly behind her as she comes back inside, so as not to make a sound.

• • •

I find him at the fourth bar. I'm surprised at my luck.

Undoing the button on his jeans, I ask him where his wife is.

He clamps a hand over my mouth and shoves me roughly into the wall, pulling my skirt up and sliding his hand into my underwear.

Where are you going dressed like that, Dave had asked.

The kid's eager. Twenty-two. All hands and a tongue that flicks awkwardly in my ear. He cums in less than a minute and stands there trembling while I re-button my blouse.

I can go down on you, he says.

Dave is sleeping when I get home, the television blue and static and buzzing in the corner. When I shut it off, he wakes. He walks up the stairs behind me, his hands on my ass.

You should wear this for me some time, he says.

When I sleep, I dream of greenbelts.

• • •

Two cop cars and a paddy wagon pull up in the middle of the afternoon. They're knocking at the door across and hauling a girl away. She's seventeen and pregnant. An oversized Coors Light T-shirt stretches across her belly, the kind you get in a case of beer.

Stop! she's screaming and more heads poke out of windows, around doorframes.

And she sees us—it's hard not to—sitting just across the street, looking and pretending not to notice.

Help me, please, she is screaming, mascara running

down her face, the officers grabbing at her arms and legs.

Dave stands and a neighbour puts a hand on his shoulder, a hand that says don't get involved. I feel him shaking beside me as he lowers himself back down and I pass him his beer. We look away because we can't take it. It's not our business, we figure, how she ended up pregnant, where her mother might be. The system is fucked, we say.

Despite the girl's condition, she is all hair and nails. A handful. It takes four of them to get her lined up to the car door before the meaty glove of a male officer grips her head and gets her into the back seat.

Jesus, one of the cops says. Christ. What a fighter.

They dust themselves from the attack as the girl kicks at the windows, dull smack after dull smack of white tennis shoe on glass.

When we get inside, I fix Dave a drink and tell him funny stories from work until he feels better, how Della broke a lightbulb in the socket and got a jolt and peed her pants that one time and how we all laughed, even her, despite the concern and the smell of burning.

We're lucky to be alive with so many objects bent on killing us, I say.

He follows me into the shower and wraps his arms around me from behind, and we stay there like that until the water gets cold and our skin shrivels.

• • •

The bride has requested that we all wear blue and that we dance in a line, like country girls at a barn dance. Barb and Minnie are ancient in taffeta. The bride's gown is designer, cut above the knee. Left foot in, left foot out. Kick, heel, turn. Kick, heel, turn, smile.

At the breaks, we are exhausted. Dave and I slip out back with his cousin, who's home from BC for the wedding.

I'm dying to see those grapes of yours, she says as she hands me the joint.

Any time. You know that.

Will you make wine this year?

Dave slips his arm around my waist and pulls me in. He smells like a man should smell, like fresh tobacco and Irish Spring and motor oil.

That's always the plan, he says.

THE WOMAN IN THE
YELLOW DRESS

THE WOMAN IN THE
YELLOW DRESS

JORGE GOT THE FIRST PICTURE when he was five. It was a gift from his grandmother, sent in the mail. It came in a long brown envelope with a red ink stamp that said Do Not Bend. His father placed it on the little easel in his room.

Jorge, he said, do you know that art is the most worthwhile pursuit?

His grandparents were painters in the old country. In the stories, this was a place where olive trees spilled over cobblestone and a clear sea stretched for miles in the distance. The picture on Jorge's easel was his first visual of that world. It was small with a porch. Tall trees splayed branches across its roof. It sat little against a big sky.

His father took a pencil and placed it in Jorge's hand over a sheet of white paper.

I want you to learn this, he said. Come downstairs when you have mastered the first window.

• • •

There's a photograph in the gallery where Jorge works the front desk. In it, a woman in a yellow dress is suspended, horizontal, a few feet over pavement. She is either flying low or she is falling, Jorge can't tell. Either way, she has his attention. He tells her he'll be back in a few moments when he goes to tidy the kitchen or post the mail. He apologizes when he leaves for lunch, says he is sorry that she cannot come, that she does not eat.

After picking up the usual items at the grocery store, Jorge finds an empty table in the deli. He sets his stuff down near the microwave and cooks the frozen dinner that promises one pound of beef and that has potatoes and a small cake that expands and bursts near the end. He eats quickly and drinks a two-litre of milk in four long gulps. He reads and re-reads Nancy's column in the paper, in which she calls the exhibit "stimulating." He tears her words out carefully, folds them into the pocket of his jeans. Jorge thinks Nancy is stimulating.

Flying and falling can look almost the same if the person is photographed at just the right moment, parallel to the ground. It's hard to tell the difference. If the arms are held out behind instead of in front or to the sides, then they are much more likely to have been flying, Jorge thinks. This is the case with the girl in the yellow dress. Then again, Jorge doesn't know much about physics or flight. This is the kind of thing that depends on so much: on trajectory and wind speed and objects of interference, unexpected forces.

Back at his desk, he hears Nancy walking through the upper wing. He hears the click of her shoes and looks up and she is not alone. Barry is there. They are talking and gesticulating and now they are looking in his direction. He takes the moment to return a phone call. Yes, Mrs.

Manchester, the opening is on schedule. Yes, it is at seven. Yes, I can meet you at the door and help you in even though you can walk perfectly well on your own and your husband will toss me dirty looks from the bar where he will take up residence for the evening, sucking back tumblers of whiskey. Looking forward to seeing you, Mrs. Manchester.

Hi, Nancy says and is in front of him.

Hi.

She raises her eyebrows.

Can I get you something? Jorge asks and smiles.

A coffee, please.

Coming right up, he says and he turns and when he does, he knocks over a stack of postcards advertising the exhibit and he feels his face go hot. He feels her there still watching and then there is the slow click of her shoes, walking from the desk.

Jorge passes the cup to her behind Barry, who is running a finger along the frame of the photograph of the girl in the yellow dress. He is up close, looking at the glass. He is saying, why do we even pay these cleaners? Nancy is rolling her eyes.

I mean, really. What are we going to do about this? Barry is on the floor now, picking up bits of paper.

Nancy looks at her watch. She says, Barry. She says, Barry, come on. Barry? It's alright. I'll talk to them.

She takes him by the arms, suggests him to his feet. They go back to their offices. Jorge pours himself a coffee. The girl in the yellow dress is looking at him, he thinks, but he can't tell for her hair.

• • •

In a letter to his parents, Jorge writes that he is fine, that he is working in the gallery, that he is perfecting his art. He seals the envelope with wax and walks it down to the mailbox and the rain is pouring. When he is home and dry, he takes out the book and looks through his work. The little house in the old country, reimagined so many times since his childhood, clear always in his mind now. A copse of olive trees. Ocean. His mother on a swing. A girl he once thought he loved.

He takes out his pencil and tries again to draw Nancy. Again, she is all heels and affected with hair and makeup. He wants to see her natural. Naked, even. In the woods. On a shoreline. As a real person. He tries to imagine what is underneath the mask she wears. He makes a few sketches that could be her, but he can't be sure. Nancy with flowing curly hair, not straightened with some iron. Nancy with white legs not tanned with some chemical spray. Maybe she is these things, and maybe she is not.

He waits near the building in the morning, as usual. He knows her habits by now. She comes home and stays in and goes to work in the morning. This is most days. A nod to the doorman, inside, a nod to the doorman, outside. Sometimes she goes to dinner or on a date, and she is different then, sure. Looser, more free. But this, too, is covered with lipstick and eyeliner and affected hair. Strange hats in the newest style.

Nancy, he imagines saying when the moment is right, I want to draw you. As you are. But he can never find the right words.

• • •

Jorge takes a walk around the gallery, puts out the postcards and assembles the little pop-up things that advertise the next show. He looks at the other pictures, reads the names of artists. There are more pictures like the woman in the yellow dress. Impossible things. Tricks of the eye. A woman falling into a wall or being thrown, and even Jorge knows that movement can't be captured like that. And a picture of a woman floating with an umbrella, kind of sideways, not in the way that a body would move. The same artist, different trick. Back as his desk, he tells the woman in the yellow dress that she is better than these other two. He tells her she is going to sell for a good price, he just knows it.

At 6:30 the caterers arrive. Jorge helps them wheel in tables and lay out white cloths and metal trays. He wears plastic gloves and arranges coconut shrimp. Like this, the sommelier says, and the waiters pour the wine, first the red and then the white and then champagne into crystal flutes that go on a separate table to be wheeled out at the right time.

Jorge greets the first three people at his desk: a man and two women. Welcome, he says, and hands them the programs. They stop at the photograph with the woman in the yellow dress.

This levitation photography, the man whispers.

It's cheap, one woman says.

I think it's interesting, the other woman says and they turn their head first to one side and then to the other, synchronized scrutiny, then the first woman says, she's suspended by a crate, it's under her belly. See how her dress looks funny right there?

Jorge looks at the woman in the yellow dress. He can

see how the dress looks funny. He can see now that her hair is moving in odd directions, as if fanned, that it's neither pulled back like she is flying nor pulled up like she is falling.

Yes, the man says. They've Photoshopped it out. I've seen the original.

The little group leaves. Jorge waits an appropriate thirty seconds before bussing the glasses. When he passes by the woman in the yellow dress he says don't mind them. It doesn't matter how you got to where you are; it only matters that you are there.

When you're falling, you are not really in the empty. There is air. You are held by air. Similarly, when you are flying, you are held by air. But this woman in the yellow, she is held not by air. She is held by a wooden crate. The rest is painted. She is neither flying nor falling. She is stuck. Suspended. Jorge feels a pang in his chest.

Mrs. Manchester and her husband and granddaughter are the last to leave. They've bought two photographs; one of them, on Jorge's suggestion, was the picture of the girl in the yellow dress. Thank you, Jorge, Mrs. Manchester says. Helpful as always. As Nancy puts the blue dot on the photograph's title tag, signifying it sold, Jorge looks away.

The doors are locked and Jorge helps the caterers pour out the leftover wine and tip trays of leftovers into garbage bags heavy with Styrofoam plates and napkins. Nancy and Barry are drunk in the upstairs office with the artists. They are smoking up there, laughing and knocking things over. Jorge is clearing away the last of the pamphlets when the party emerges, goes barrelling out the door. He is about to lock the door when he hears the click of Nancy's shoes on the stairs behind him.

Good night, Jorge, she says, as she passes and he flushes hot. She said his name. He holds the door for her and watches as her cab pulls away.

• • •

He draws the mountains again. They are the same each time.

Jorge will live in the mountains someday, he has decided. He will take a knapsack with sharp knives and make his own tent and make his own life there, in the quiet. Live with the animals. Watch over the old country.

His father has written to say they would like to visit, and Jorge has seen his apartment truly for the first time. Its little furniture, its lack of life. Just a few drawings tacked to the walls, and always the same. The Nancys, the mountains, the small family house.

He writes back to say this is not a good time, but he does not post the letter. He walks past the mailbox, he doesn't know why. He finds himself at the gallery door. He finds himself standing in the light of early morning in front of the woman in the yellow dress, struck by the lie of her. How someone could stick her there like that. Make it look as though she is moving when she is stuck. How the girl must have hurt during the photo shoot, staying still like that for maybe hours. He wants to tell her he is sorry, but he doesn't know how to find her.

He takes his pocket knife and cuts the photograph, corner to corner.

• • •

Nancy is standing at his desk when he arrives at open.

Someone has vandalized the place. The security tapes were off. Do you know anything about this?

Jorge stands beside her. I don't know what could have happened, he tells Nancy.

We're going to pay dearly for this, she says.

It is his job to call Mrs. Manchester and deliver the news. The photographer can easily produce another copy, he says, it will take just a week.

It is all fake anyway, he wants to say. Nothing worthwhile should be so easily made again.

The gallery is quiet all day, so he dusts, and makes extra coffee rounds. Nancy has locked her office door and does not want to be disturbed. She doesn't understand how someone could do such a thing. Ruin a lovely piece of art. She doesn't want to see anyone. She doesn't want any coffee.

The next day at lunch, she is at his desk again, and Barry is with her. The man who owns the newsstand across the road saw Jorge enter the building early in the morning, hours before opening. He saw Jorge slash the photograph.

Nancy looks at him with some kind of hate.

They wait until he packs his things and watch him to the door, without another word.

• • •

Nancy doesn't leave for work. Jorge checks his watch. He gets another coffee from the shop, keeping a close watch on the doorman, but she does not emerge.

Maybe, he thinks, he has broken her heart.

If she would just come out, he could tell her this, but

she doesn't come out. He touches the folded photograph in his bag. The girl with the yellow dress, stuck now forever. By noon, he has tired of the watch and heads home, to the little desk by the window, and this time, when he tries to draw Nancy, he cannot find her. He has lost her.

A letter arrives that says things like terminated and costs for damages and it has her signature.

Jorge holds his head in his hands.

He takes his keys and he lets himself into the gallery. Stands in Nancy's office for a while, then takes the steps to the rooftop patio two by two.

The night is clear and the smog has thinned, revealing stars. Six storeys below, there is the buzz of nightclub bass, the sharp sweep of disco lights. Warbled conversations spill into the streets and into the backseats of cabs that speed and stop and ferry people off to late-night booty calls and all-night pizza joints. A man is singing some old Irish song, zig-zagging through lineups, and girls are giggling, shuffling nervously in mini-dresses that blow up with the wind.

Jorge steps to the edge but does not look down. This, he has decided, is key. He takes one deep breath and then another. He dangles a foot over the edge to let the height play with his senses, then he pulls the foot back. He takes a deep breath, closes his eyes and pushes off to fly or to fall.

THE PHONEBOOK

THE PHONEBOOK

THEY LEFT THE PHONEBOOK ON the step on a rainy April day and by the time I arrived home, it was soaked right through. I didn't want to drag it into the house, all wet like that and dripping water everywhere. I imagined the thick gluey pages drying to deformity on my kitchen table. So I pushed it to the farthest corner of the bottom step, over under the mailbox where it might not be noticed, and I went inside.

From then on I saw it whenever I left and whenever I arrived home. I felt the eyes of cab drivers scan it while they waited for me to lock the door, its distinct yellowness blazing against the drab grey of the row-house siding.

Weeks passed and there was no improvement in the state of it. Large drops of whitened water clung to the inside of the plastic, toxic and waiting.

After a while, people started asking questions.

Just throw it out, they said.

A few offered to get rid of it for me, if that would help.

It's just a phonebook, I said. I can do it myself.

One friend found it funny. That's priceless, he said. I should take a picture of that, he said, but he never got around to it.

It was one of the small injustices of the world, I figured, that it had been left outside on such a rainy day. It couldn't come in now. It couldn't really go anywhere else. It was a dud. It had been pissed on by the universe. It was too late, soaked with water from a dozen more rains and snowfalls, and there were probably earwigs.

Besides, I couldn't easily lift the weight of those drenched and dirty pages with all of those names and numbers, thousands of them, bogging it down.

And if I took it in now, it would cause a stir. People would be wondering why the sudden move and I would find myself having to explain. Someone would feel justified that I bent to the quiet neighbourly pressure and hauled the thing indoors.

One day some men came by to replace the front door with a new door; a man and his father. I offered them tea, but they declined. Instead, they told me stories about how they knew my landlord and how the house had been built. I watched as they ripped down the old doorframe and hammered nails into fresh new plywood. When the work was done, there was sawdust and other debris that they swept up and laid outside in bags.

The next morning, they came by while I was sleeping and took the garbage away. When I left the house a while later, I saw the phonebook was gone. There was just the outline of where it had once sat and, inside of that, the cleanest part of the step.

MR. MORIARITY

MR. MORIARITY

MR. MORIARITY

HERE. COUNT THEM OUT.

1. I have not loved enough.

My first time was with a girl in my Grade 11 class. I walked her home and she said to come in, that her parents were out, and we sat on the couch and then she straddled me and she said put it in and I did, and it was over fast. I couldn't look her in the eye after that. Then she married a buddy of mine and I couldn't look him in the eye either, afraid of their pillow talk, afraid of how much longer he lasted than me.

At twenty-four, I was serviced in a back alley by a waitress in the place I tended bar. I shouldn't be saying this at all, but there's no better time and so never mind it anyway. I'm dying. I can say whatever I want. At night here looking up at the ceiling I think of that waitress. How it was just as I imagined sex would be when I was a boy. No sweating and awkwardness, no babies as consequence. Just a quick thing in an alleyway. Order up.

Margaret and I had fun. You can't talk about that stuff,

ever. It's not the same with a wife, what you can and can't say. She was funny, too, Margaret. Boy, did we have fun. Truth be told, most of the fun came when we got older and pudgier and it didn't matter anymore about things hanging out where there shouldn't be. Margaret would say, bring those sexy liver spots to bed, old timer, and once when we were drinking, she said to choke her a little bit. So I did. A minute later, I felt her go all slack. Took a full five minutes to wake her up and all she said was jeez, b'y, what'd you go and do that for?

Love and sex aren't the same thing. There was plenty of loving, but still it is true that I never loved enough. Not nearly enough. Or I never loved enough out loud. I loved the idea of love, like in the movies. I loved that first girl who married my buddy, even after she got all thin and angry from cancer treatments later on, even though I couldn't look her in the eye. I loved her for climbing onto me like that, when I was so young and afraid, for showing me what it was to be fearless, to wander. I loved that waitress and her mouth. I loved Margaret for being young and beautiful and having my children and raising my children and for her pot roast and her father's summer cabin and the boat he left me when he died, how he was like my father too, and how she smelled most of the time, faint rose or lavender, nothing too strong, not like perfume, just off the skin. Natural. I loved that she knew me, who I was. How she folded the laundry. Of course, I didn't tell her any of this. It just wasn't what you did in those days. And when she died, they put me in here.

Here people say did you have a wife and I say yes, and her name was Margaret and she was beautiful and they nod and they smile and they say it's an awful shame, getting old, and I say yes, it sure is.

In the beginning, I thought of her often. Everything was different, sleeping alone and eating alone and nobody to talk to about the little things, how was your day and that sort of stuff. The smell of her faded too and I almost can't imagine it anymore. Now it's just me and the memory of Margaret and the children who don't come by, except on Christmas and my birthday, and that is why I don't love them.

• • •

I'm at that age where embarrassing things happen, and falling asleep in the common room is just the beginning. There's no point in telling you and ruining the surprise. You'll know when you get older. I write letters to my son. He calls on Sundays. My daughter doesn't call at all but I keep pictures of the both of them on the nightstand for folks to admire. It's important to have family.

When Mrs. Mindy down the hall died, there was a kerfuffle. I guess it's on my mind because it just happened. I mean, it's not the first time somebody kicked the bucket in this place. In fact, it's practically a regular event. Someday my turn will come.

Anyway, Mrs. Mindy went out kicking and screaming. Greta was in some state about it. Ran bawling down the hallway like a little girl and she's the tough kind, the used-to-seeing-people-die kind you wouldn't think to be bothered. Mrs. Mindy said fuck this and fuck that and fuck you to everyone who came near her. She threw a bedpan full of piss at the nurses. She shouted take me out of this godforsaken place, Christ willing, and we all heard it down in the common room, right in the middle of a quiet Wednesday afternoon. It was something. And Mrs. Mindy such a lovely lady the rest of the time. I'm sure she wouldn't have guessed that. She didn't know what was happening, I'm sure. They called the priest in for last rights and then he came around to see us too, on account of us overhearing.

Father, I said to him, I don't give a good flying fuck (yep, I mean it—that's what I said) about her yelling and screaming. She had every right, far as I could tell. Sure, that could happen to anybody.

God bless you, he said, and went on to the next person.

I built my first house when I was twenty-four, just back from overseas. I loved every board that went into the place, got paid next to nothing. I told Margaret all about it in the evenings. I think she was probably driven off her head at me. Get on with ya, b'y, she'd say. Order me out of the kitchen. I knew, though, right then and there that it was the thing for me. So I went and got my trade and I started my own business, building houses. I called it Buddy and Son, because that's what people say, hey buddy, some house you're building there. See my meaning?

At Christmas time, the thing to do was to drive around town looking at the lights. Margaret made hot chocolate in a pot and we took mugs and all, piled into the car. We drove right slow, seeing who had what on their lawns, reindeers and Santa Clauses and the like. And I said I built this house or that house and when the kids were old enough they asked questions about how and we all sung "Silent Night" and "Jingle Bells" and that became a tradition. Often we finished the last verse pulled up in the driveway, Margaret not letting anybody out of the car until it was done. Tradition, she said, was important.

I built houses for young families and old families and single mothers and single men with close male friends who lived together and were never seen in town, though we all knew what was going on. Sometimes, I'd be driving along and see something was changed and I'd get out and have a look. They'd come out sometimes and say, Mr. Moriarity, what are you doing down there, when I was poking at the foundation or some such. Just checking up on things, I'd say, and I kept in touch with most of the homeowners like that. Sometimes they called me in for renovations and it was funny, seeing your house long afterwards, when it had been lived in for so long, how it felt like the family, how there was a hole in a wall or a break in a staircase. Before they took my license, I used to do house-check runs. I'd go right through town and check on every house, sometimes go right up to the windows. Caught Mrs. St. Croix in her skivvies one time, but she never knew, thank God.

Nothing comes on television that we can all agree on. We sit out in the common room most evenings and watch the local station after the news. Game shows, sitcoms. Everybody cheers when somebody gets a word on *Wheel of Fortune*. Have you seen that show? I recommend it. Win some money on it, too, if you can get yourself on there.

• • •

2. I did not travel enough.

I've been to all of the provinces in Canada, but none of the territories. And I have never seen Toronto, though I lived in Ontario for six months once on a forestry project with my brother. I've seen Ottawa and Montreal and Vancouver and Calgary and Edmonton. One of my daughters lives in Toronto and says come visit, you always wanted to come here, there's a spare room, but she doesn't understand how hard it is at my age to fly, how it wouldn't be fun now, Toronto, how that moment has been lost so far as I'm concerned. She sends me little brochures from places like the CN Tower and playbills from shows they take in because she thinks I like theatre.

I was away once and that was in Europe for war and it's not the same as travelling when you're shit-baked and twenty-three and just hoping to get the fuck home. There are no tourist maps, no fancy hotels.

Here comes Greta with my pills. She says, Mr. Moriarity, what is it you're writing? She says this is the most writing I've ever seen you do, Mr. Morarity. I say, Greta, don't you mind that at all and I take the pills and she watches to ensure I swallow each one.

• • •

Margaret was seventy-eight when I found her on the kitchen floor. She'd raised two babies and had a job at the general grocer for twenty-three years, checking people in and giving out lottery tickets. She once broke her foot trying to do the foxtrot and it never healed right, but that was it until then. She'd had cancer in her stomach and never knew it. They said that's what took her. That and the age, which was to be expected, they said.

I don't know what to expect of age. Sometimes I feel like I'm shouting into darkness, abyss. Sometimes I feel like I am not shouting at all. We are all prisoners, I guess. Here, they give you stuff, they take stuff away. It's funny how we return to childhood. I think I expected something different. But I'm alive. That's what I tell myself. You are either living, or you are dying.

I'll tell you why people held captive keep track of time with sticks or small marks on walls. Time is important. Time keeps you grounded. It gives the mind something to spring from, to work with. I was a prisoner of war for a short time in Europe. Held in a pit in the ground for thirty-two days. And down there in the pit there was no time. Down there in the pit with lice crawling on your skin, standing in filth, you start to think of things.

I thought of bathing, of Margaret bathing. We were young then but I knew her in that way already. It wasn't a fantasy I'd had for a long time, since I was a boy, having known women, but when you are dirty you fantasize clean.

I imagined the air thick with soap and perfumes. Water so hot that when you put your feet in it hurt, that you have to take them out again and test with your hand. I thought of Margaret at home sinking into this hot bath, putting her foot in and taking it out, adjusting, doing it again. Maybe her hair was in curlers and she would close her eyes and allow herself to drift off for a few minutes. She might have the radio on. She might run a hand down the softness of her arm with a wash cloth. She might shave her legs. Afterwards, she would stand, her breasts shedding the water in sheets. The white hairs would stand against her tanned belly. She would wrap herself in a warm towel and tuck the outside layer into the inside layer to keep in place. . Maybe she'd wipe a hand across the steamed mirror to see as she applied lotion to her face, her neck. I could smell the scene. It was so when I came back from the dream, I realized again where I was fully, in the stench and the dark with the dead and dying men, and I would try to dream again.

When I got home and I was feeling well enough, I couldn't shake it. I said, Margaret, can you let me watch you in the bathtub. When she raised her eyebrows I said just do this for me, please and so she did. Margaret could get clean but I couldn't. I would scrub and scrub but nothing changed. I never could get the stink of that place off. I could smell it always and I believed for a long time that Margaret could smell it, too.

Sometimes I feel like I am shouting into the abyss and then I realize that I am not, that I am sitting in a chair overlooking the lawn and there's Mrs. Devon with her young granddaughter who visits every week and who is so polite and who says hello to everyone and sometimes stays for dinner and for *Wheel of Fortune*. You see cars moving off in the distance on the freeway and you wonder if one will turn down the long drive, you can see it coming for a while, and pull into a parking space. Maybe somebody will get out, maybe my son and his wife and that baby of his. Maybe they'll sit with you for a few minutes and ask how things are. Maybe they'll bring some sort of treat from town, croissants or a bucket of fried chicken.

Greta's uniform is blue with ducks on it. It used to be

that nurses wore white and stockings and padded white shoes that squeaked. Now they wear sneakers.

Bring me my paper, would you, dear Greta, I say in my best voice.

Sure thing, Mr. M. she says.

Got a boyfriend yet?

Nope, not yet.

Keep me in mind, will ya?

Will do.

And Greta is off down the hall. She'll be back soon enough. She comes more and more to the room.

• • •

3. I never followed my dreams.

When you are young, they give you dreams. Ideas of you being this and you being that. They let you see yourself as something great. You can imagine standing in the centre spotlight, playing to a full house on an old acoustic, you know, one with a proper story, one that's taken a proper beating. I think of that Country Joe and the Fish song about boys coming home in a box. How you put down your books and pick up a gun. Well, it's more than that, too. You put down your books and you pick up a wife and a few kids, a mortgage, a car payment. You move the books into an old bookshelf next to the easy chair next to the TV that becomes the centre of your world, your distraction. Your wife puts her dreams away, too. Replaces them with children and shelf liners and Sunday dinners. You all do the things you are supposed to do and you don't ask questions. Questions are for the end.

I knew from the time I was a little boy that I wanted to be a cowboy. I know how it sounds, but I'm quite serious. I'm not talking about just wearing a hat and boots and riding around on a horse all day, I'm talking mending fences and barn roofs, tending to land and to cattle. I owned three Newfoundland ponies in the eighties. They were willed to me by an elderly neighbour, and I loved the three of them until they died, but it wasn't exactly the same thing.

• • •

On sunny days they bring us to the porch. One of the nurses slathers our faces and arms with a thick cream to protect us from the sun. If it's Greta, I say can you do it again, and she winks at me. She says, you're good there, Mr. Moriarity.

Today a wasp crawled up from the grass. I watched his slow progress. He makes it nearly to my chair, making me anxious, and then he falls on his side and then onto his back. I've never seen a wasp face. Mostly I kill the little buggers when they get into the house. Women aren't too fond. But this one had my sympathy. He lay there, body pulsing, antennae wiggling, waiting to die. Someone said there was a nest down by the gardener's shed. They laid out some sugary treats and they came in hoards, the wasps. This one must have been out. The maintenance man brought a bottle into the nurses station, showing how many had died, then he cut the nest down with an axe.

• • •

4. I never got the car

I know it sounds silly, but I had my eye on a few over the years. Imagined spinning down some highway, radio loud, free as a bird. But the kind of cars I loved weren't built for family. When you're married, you stop being a person in some ways. Become part of a unit. You make money and put shingles on a house, you paint. Everything is for everybody else. I sat in the den and looked at pictures in magazines from car dealerships. I kept picking the things up, not sure why. There was always some feature I wanted and at least that, I figured, could be accommodated. And when it wasn't, when I didn't get what I wanted, and I looked at Margaret and how her hair was frayed and how she wasn't a girl any longer and how much she had given up, I figured enough, stop being a shitheel. But then I still kind of wonder what it would have been like to drive a brand new car off the lot and have her paid for.

• • •

It's all a jumble in the end. You look back and you try to pull on those moments that you should remember. The wedding day. The birth of the children. Retirement. But life is not that simple. The moments are yours for the choosing, aren't they? You should write things down.

Our wedding was at a little church in the town where we were raised and there were maybe forty people. The night before I was not allowed to see the bride and my friends threw a bachelor party in the basement of a house and a grainy video played on the rabbit-eared television that showed a woman stripping her clothes off while standing on a bed in a motel room. The boys said I was in chains now. I played darts and as the night wore on I couldn't even hit the board and I left lamenting the fresh wounds in the wall and promising to help him plaster when I got back. I remember stopping on my way home when my stomach roiled and I saw the stretch of my life ahead with this one woman and I wondered was she enough and was I enough and I sat on a rock overlooking the harbour and listened to the waves and felt the change coming, that tomorrow I would be a man. My father was waiting for me when I got home with advice that was: never raise a hand in anger, give credit where credit is due, and hold up your end of the bargain, whatever about the rest of them.

The first child was not birthed in an instant, but in agonizing hours. Thirty-six of them while I worked my hands alone, in another room. She didn't want me there and it wasn't yet the fashion anyway. I drank coffee and paced and Margaret screamed and yelled in the next room and I cursed myself for doing it to her and wondered if the whole thing would ruin her lady parts. I did. I imagined what things would look like down there now, and how long it would be before she would let me at them again (six months on the first, and eight on the second). The doctor sent me out to get more towels and to walk along the shore and then to gather the family and to eat food and I said when is this going to be over and they said don't yell and it will all work itself out, stuff like that. There was a long stretch of silence when I thought she was dead and I found myself crying in my mother's arms and she was laughing at me first and then she was tucking me into a bed full of blankets saying, there, there, baby, you're just exhausted.

Try and get some rest. I woke and had more coffee and went for cigarettes and, sometime after I came back, the doctor came out and this time he was holding something that was wriggling and my son was in my arms and I had never felt so much joy in my life, it bowled me over. I looked over his little hands and face and I made a million promises and he gurgled and it was the best thing I had ever seen, the absolute best thing.

• • •

5. I never learned enough

I missed most things. The truth being the main thing. The news. The revelations. The information. How could you keep up anyway? There's so much floating around out there, you'd never stop learning it all. It's like, I know that word but not the truth of it, not the truth of words or the truth of you. Heck, I don't even know the truth of me.

When I was a boy my mother said I would be strong and tall, she could tell because of my long arms and how I drank too much milk, but I grew to be five foot fuck all and in school they made fun of me, called me stump. So for a while I thought I'd play hockey or baseball, but it turned out I wasn't good at those things.

I was going to be an insurance salesman like my father and make money door to door but I didn't have the wit for it, I couldn't lie. And so the money never came and I never had the house and maybe the house didn't matter. Don't get me wrong, I had a house, just not the house, the one with the spires and the fenced grounds and the swimming pool and the tennis court.

In 1992, I had a Workers' Comp claim on account of my back and I couldn't work for eight months and I read the entire *Encyclopedia Britannia* from cover to cover, including all that was written on the maps and the entire index, and four years' worth of *National Geographic*. But besides that I never had an education. Just Grade 9 and the ways of the world, as my father would say, and that was all she wrote.

Remember being young and possible. That was grand. I wish Margaret was here.

Oh, Margaret. Are we young up there?

I imagine her. Not wearing the lace dress on our wedding day or naked and dripping from a bath but in a green satin dress she wore to Robert's high-school graduation. She was forty-two. Her hair was done up on top of her head, her lips red.

Mr. Moriarity, Greta says. It's time for supper.

STAYS A BEAR

STAYS A BEAR

THERE ISN'T MUCH IN THE way of ice cream, Jesse says.

She's leaning into the frozen cooler, the tips of her hair brushing the Klondike Bars and Strawberry Shortcakes. So we walk the extra block to Stinson's for cones. Her bell bottoms trail the sidewalk, sweeping dirt. They are a soft sky blue, velvet corduroy. She holds my hand and somebody waves and she waves back. It's a boy who looks important, carrying books. The cone drips pink and sticky down over my hand and onto my T-shirt.

Quick, she says. Before it dries.

We stop on the sidewalk in front of a lawn. Jesse wets a cloth in a sprinkler, uses it to wash my face, to sop up the ice cream. She puts the cloth in a sandwich bag. These are things she carries in her backpack. She puts them away and takes my hand and we walk again, and there is a spot of wet growing above the Care Bear rainbow on my shirt.

• • •

At 6:45, the doorbell rings. I know because I've been watching the clock. Today Jesse wears a dress that's brown with white flowers. It's thin, the material of the dresses that hang in Mom's closet. Jesse smiles at me while they give her the instructions, same drill: restaurant phone number, neighbour's number. There are chips in the cupboard, but none for me after supper. She nods yes. I slip my hand into hers and she takes it without looking, and when the door closes behind them she says c'mon, let's go, and we run to the living room and my ponytail does windmills and we fall to the floor laughing. She takes the boxes with board games out from under the coffee table.

Let's play, she says.

It's Hungry Hungry Hippos and I win three times. Then she makes hot chocolate and we play checkers at the table, and she turns the board over at the end and reminds me what a rook is and how you move the horse and I say but I don't want to play chess and she says you will someday, and that it's important to learn things.

Are you smart? I ask and she laughs as she drops the pieces into the box and we walk it across the room together and slide it under the couch, though either of us could have done it ourselves.

Farrah Fawcett has hair that's feathered like a bird, but I don't think she looks like a bird at all. I like the show still.

Are you okay to watch this? Jesse asks. I think she knows I will watch whatever she wants but I nod anyway and she brings me popcorn in a giant glass bowl and presses one finger to her lips that says, shhh, don't tell your mom. And the girls get their instructions from Charlie and they're off, and we scrape the last kernels along the thick butter that sticks to the bottom and we wash the bowl together and put it back in the cupboard before we walk upstairs to my room.

The stairs creak every few. Jesse is ahead of me, her legs netted in pantyhose. She turns the lamp on and closes the curtains. She says which book and I say the fairytales and she says that's a big one while I snuggle my way into a good spot on the pillow with Sam, so he can hear too. Jesse reads once upon a time and turns the pages and soon I shut my eyes and I am dreaming that we are walking on a seashore, Jesse and me and a fat baby that falls over again and again and when I laugh Jesse says no, don't laugh, that's my baby, that's your sister. I wake up with a sob stuck in my throat and when it lets loose it's like a cough and I think I hear Mom say something to Dad in their room so I cry into the pillow where they won't know.

Come here in the morning, I whisper to Sam, pretending it's Jesse. Sam says nothing, stays a bear.

• • •

Mom and I go to the mall and I have to wait on a bench while she tries on dresses. She doesn't ask me if I like them, but the blonde lady tells her what she thinks. They make you look curvy, she says. Not a day over twenty. Green is your colour.

The man waiting for his wife tries to talk to me, but I say no, that he's a stranger. He nods and smiles like I'm stupid or something, so I turn the page and look at the dinosaurs and then I drop Sam on the floor by accident. Mom says, Pick that up! and it's then that I see Jesse, walking with a boy toward the door to outside. He has a hand in a back pocket of her jeans, right on her bum. I slip off the bench and run to catch her but they're too fast and she doesn't hear me yell her name. When I get to the glass, my mother is behind me in a dress with the tags still on, and behind her the blonde lady from the store, and my mother is shaking me, where are you going? What did I tell you?

Jesse steps into a blue sports car, and puts her bare feet on the dashboard, wiggles her painted toenails. She is smoking a cigarette. Not wearing a seat belt. They drive off in a cloud of rock music and I hum the tune for the rest of the day at supper and through movie night and I am scolded and sent to bed early, without a story.

• • •

That Wednesday, Mom goes unexpectedly out and Jesse shuts the door and we watch, peeking through the curtains, as the car pulls out of the driveway. Dad's at work until ten.

She has an album in her backpack and we play it loud and make milkshakes in the kitchen. She winds the chord around her finger while she talks to Marcus.

Is Marcus your boyfriend?

Yes, she says.

I saw you in the mall.

She giggles into the phone. Can I have some nail polish? I ask.

Her friend Irene is on the couch. They have cotton balls between their toes. Jesse walks to her backpack, her toes spread and pointing up.

Don't tell your parents, okay?

I say I won't.

Jesse finds the bottle and Irene stands behind me, brushing my hair. Jesse says put your foot up here and I do and she stretches my toes far, far apart and stuffs cotton in between. One small bead of red paint slides down the brush and onto my big toe, and I laugh but it doesn't tickle like I thought and anyway Jesse uses the brush to flatten it out. Just like that it is glossy and perfect and done but don't touch it, she says. Each fat toe pad flattens between her fingers and each nail comes back coloured, changed, like it can't ever be undone. When they're dry, I'm allowed to walk.

For the rest of the evening I put my feet on different things to see how they look: the coffee table, the grey tile in the bathroom, the comforter on my bed. We wash the dishes in the kitchen after Irene leaves and we spray smelly stuff to take away the smoke smell and then she says, shit, I'm so stoned, and she starts giggling and she can't stop so I tell her that joke about the firemen and the priest and that makes her laugh more, and when she tucks me in she smiles and she says, you're such a card.

She is out the door as Dad is coming up the walk. She is giggling and skipping, accepting a twenty.

• • •

She's not coming, Mom says, and Mrs. Johnson's Glenda comes instead. She wears old lady dresses and makes me watch *Dallas* and she tucks me in at nine. I am hungry, my stomach rolling. I sneak down the stairs to the kitchen where Glenda is on the phone with her mother.

I'm fine, she says.

She's in bed.

Watching *Dallas*.

Do I have to?

I don't want to.

C'mon, Mom.

I pause on the stair that creaked and Glenda stops talking and pokes her head around the corner.

Back to bed, kiddo, she says and tries a smile.

I turn and climb the stairs back to my room. I crawl back into bed with Sam.

Glenda comes up later and turns off the light. Her glasses reflect the streetlight from outside my window. Goodnight, she whispers, but I pretend to be sleeping, my eyes nearly closed.

Mom and Dad are arguing, getting out of the car. When the door opens downstairs, I creep out to hear Glenda saying yes, all went well and yes, she thinks she would like to babysit me from now on.

That's wonderful, Mom says. She was good?

Yes, Glenda says. She got out of bed the one time, though.

Mom says she will talk with me in the morning. I get back in bed and pull the covers over my face and rub the polished toenails of the one foot against the sole of the other foot, feeling for red.

OVER SOME THING

OVER SOME THING

ONE TIME THEY ARGUED AND Charlie took off and drove all over the city, her at home worrying. He made it halfway out the parkway before the car sputtered and died. He managed to pull off the road and he called her from the soldier statue to come and get him out of the rain and to bring some gas. She said to fuck off and hung the phone up in his face.

At the party, Charlie describes what happened next. I beat the receiver to bits, he says. It just came apart in my hand. Then I looked out at the car just sitting there, her car, no fucking good to me now, sure, and so I went over to the side of the road and I picked up this big rock and I let loose, man. I smashed the passenger window first. This feeling was going down my arms. Like liquid. Like I'd been injected with something.

He clenches his fists, his hair gone all wild and fraying across his forehead. He's always sweating at this part, getting riled up.

I smashed all the windows. By the time I got to the windshield, I was soaked to the skin and froze, too. I just hit it and hit it and hit it and hit it, and then one car went by, and then another, and before I knew it there were news vans and I was on my way to the cop shop and I had to call my mother—imagine, a grown man of thirty!—to come and pick me up because me and the wife had a fight.

Charlie looks at her here and everyone laughs. A few aww and a few twist up their mouths disapprovingly. The crowd disperses. Charlie slips his arm around her waist. It is them and Grim, the owner of the house, and Grim says he doesn't know how Charlie gets away with these things.

They drink their wine and Charlie chats up a business-man in a crumpled suit and when they leave through the back door, they have to dash for the car so they don't get wet. In the front seat Charlie kisses her slowly, holding his mouth on hers, his lips cold and firm. They take the long way home. The rain pellets the ocean.

For a while, they sit in the driveway. The kids are in bed. She pays the babysitter.

Later they fight in the bedroom over some thing that isn't really what the fight is about and he storms down the stairs, making a big fuss and leaving her to sleep alone. She hears him down there pacing and grunting like an animal, trying to decide what to do with his anger. In the morning they dance avoidance in the kitchen making eggs and toast and before he leaves he says, bye baby, I'll see you at supper.

• • •

One morning in June, she walks into his office to offer him a cup of coffee and he is weeping in his leather-back chair. He had been doing origami, he told her later when she had him in the bathtub, stuffed full of Ativan and Tetley. He happened to read on one of the packages that the paper was handmade. The thought, he said, of little Chinese hands—probably children in sweatshops—was too much for him and he started bawling, and that was when she'd found him.

Jesus fucking Christ, Charlie, she said. It's the Japanese, not the Chinese. Don't stay in there til you're a prune.

The doctor prescribed Zoloft and a week off of work so he could amble about in a bathrobe and not shower, get caught underfoot. She sent him to the store for cigarettes and bread and he seemed happy for something to do. Sometimes he'd be gone an hour or more and would come back with tales of sad beggars or stray cats. In every story, he was the hero. He bought Halls for a coughing drunk outside Needs; healer of the sick. When a mother cried out, Sally? he'd replied, Here she is! and walked the girl back to her mother. At the end of the week, their bank account was short forty bucks because he'd made a loan to Roy who wanted to get his life back on track and who would pay them back, he had their address. A week later, as the police assessed the damage from the break-in, Charlie tried Roy's phone number and got the Sally Ann instead. The message said Christmas ornaments, two-for-one.

On a Monday he was back to work and happy to be out of the house. On Wednesday, when she saw the blood, she fainted. She came to on the carpet, the dog licking her face. In the moment before she got the strength to stand, she thought of the kids and how they might wake.

Charlie?

Charlie was face down on the bed, a long jagged cut on his forearm dripping blood to the floor. He was dead weight. Put pressure on it, she thought and got up, got to the phone. Joan at 9-1-1 said stay with him.

The front door broke after three kicks and cost two hundred dollars to replace.

• • •

I'm alone.

You're not alone. I'm here.

I'm still alone.

Even with me here.

Even with you here.

Charlie chews slowly on the potatoes, like a cow mawing on grass. She forgets now what it means for him to chew normally. He's so pale from the indoors.

• • •

They don't talk about the episode at Christmas, only enough to name it that: the episode. His mother whispers the word to her in the kitchen, cautioning. All through dinner, Charlie tells stories of work: units sold, pretty sales girls, hotels.

His father wants to know how the new car is doing.

Great, Charlie says, and puts his hand on hers on the table. We put $5k down. She rides like a dream.

After supper, they strap into the seat belts and drive around the block a few times. She's in the back with the mother, but they keep to their own sides, watch out their own windows. The neighbourhood is quiet under white, packed snow. One of the houses doesn't have Christmas lights and they take guesses about where they've gone off to, Aruba or Tampa or somewhere with a spa that pampers you for the whole twelve days.

· · ·

It's the third number in the book. Yes, he says. I can meet you at three.

Laura takes a cab to the scrapyard. At the gates, a man meets her on an ATV and she rides sidesaddle to the back of the lot.

Take your pick, he says.

Are you sure it's okay?

Have at 'er, he says.

When she pulls the crowbar from her bag, he steps back.

She starts with the back passenger window. It takes a long time. The man smokes a cigarette. He disappears for a while and comes back with two milk crates and two cans of coke. When the glass cracks, she finds a kind of rhythm. She keeps on smashing until the last sliver falls from the frame, then she drops the crowbar and hops around, all full of adrenaline. The man is clapping. Laura drinks the coke in three gulps and burps and the man laughs at this too and claps some more.

You're one strange lady, he says, and it strikes them both funny and they laugh harder than they should, he on his milk crate, her doubled over with the crowbar across her knees.

She takes out the tail lights. The ground is a carpet of sparkling white glass.

They have tea at the man's house, where pictures of his dead wife line the mantel, and he drives her back on the ATV and she rides the right way and she wonders what she was thinking the first time.

The cab driver waits, relieved, as she runs back to give the man the crowbar. The streets to home are quiet and warm in the sunshine and children play on the lawns, in the shadows.

PEANUTS OR COOKIES

PEANUTS OR COOKIES

THE BROCHURE PROMISES PARADISE. JOAN picks one from the bottom of the stack, unbent and sleek. Runs her hands over stretches of white sand beaches, gathers together her photocopies and goes around to Sally's cubicle.

I have an idea, she says.

Sally swings around in her chair and snatches the little ad. She eyes the clear ocean backdrop, the local people tanning on the beach, surfing the waves, serving the drinks. Like jewels, their deep-toned, crystal skin. Like in the movies.

She fixes a look at Joan, at her gleeful excitement. She hands back the brochure and swivels back to her screen.

I can't afford it, she says.

Joan takes a seat in the chair reserved for clients. Lets out a sigh. At any moment, Mr. Carny could come by, shoo them like chickens.

But we just got our bonuses, Joan says. I think this is just what we need.

Sally makes a little grunt.

If it's a matter of money, Joan says, I'll pay for the tickets. We can work it out later. Or someday, you can take me on a trip.

Come on, Sally, she says. When have we ever done anything adventurous?

The bus is rattling up 1st Avenue when Joan's phone rings Sally. The next morning, waiting in reception to plead their case, Joan has to tell Sally three times to stop tapping her foot.

For a long time, Mr. Carny considers the brochure, and the idea of a girls' trip, whatever that means. And when Joan stands to give her little speech about employee wellness, she feels his eyes scan her body, settle on her belly. Probably imagining her mid-life crisis spreading wide over a bikini bottom. Probably reminding himself to be kind to his elders.

I'm fifty-five years old, Mr. Carny. I've never had a vacation in my life, Joan says. And quite frankly, we've both earned it.

He softens a little, turns the glossy pictures over in his hands. Sally shifts in her chair, clears her throat.

Paradise, hey? He shakes his head. You girls enjoy.

• • •

Walking through the airport with her brand new set of designer luggage and her boarding pass, Joan feels at ease. The stewardess says welcome to Island Air and there's some local drum music playing over the PA as they are given instruction about what to do if the plane goes down. Somehow, there they are, her and Sally, choosing between peanuts and cookies. Miles from home.

Sally has donned this straw hat they sold her at the airport shop. She looks like a lovely witch. She says take my picture, and makes her best vacation face as Joan tries to figure out the flash on her phone. When they land, Sally posts it to Twitter, with the hashtags #firstvacation #islandbound #iquitmyjob.

But you didn't, Joan points out.

Not yet, Sally says, stepping out into the sunlight. But I'm tempted.

At the gates, you form a line and wait for the soldiers to wave you through. Joan is putting zinc oxide on her nose, a long, creamy strip of it that stands out against her freckled skin. Sally says something about the humidity and swats a fly.

Up front, the tour guides are waving people through, four and five at a time, and getting them on the bus.

Sally does what she says she wasn't going to do and brings up the guns. She shifts nervously, watches the soldiers. No man's land, they jokingly refer to it on tourist sites.

Shhh, Joan tells her. Try not to think about it. Everyone has to go through here.

Shaking her head, she takes the lead past the line of guards and into the bus and, at the top of the three stairs, almost knocks into a tall, bare-chested Islander. Behind her, Sally gasps.

The man reaches out a hand, helps Joan up the final stair. Another Islander, a woman, leads them to their seats. Someone places drinks in their hands.

We should do this more often, Sally whispers. I've never seen a man like that before!

Don't be racist, Joan says.

She nods her head against the window. All that prep. All that heat. The warm white sand waiting on the other side of the barrier for her to sink her toes in. She dozes off for a while. When she wakes, Sally is clutching her arm.

Did you hear that?

Joan can see they've stopped, the alarm on the face of the driver. We're not at the beach yet, Sally says.

The attractive young Islander guides in their Islander getups are moving into the aisle. The volume on the speakers pulses local dance vibes through the back of Joan's seat. The Islanders lean their soft, exotic bodies over the rows of tourists, their long, muscled arms pulling down velvet curtains. A haze of smoke or sex, Joan can't tell which, floats in the air, bluish grey, just visible. She wouldn't swear to it, but outside, a spurt of machine gun fire maybe.

A male guide stretches a large hand out to take hers, leads her to her feet. Around his neck, a string with wood beads that reads P-E-A-C-E. For a moment, for the first time in Joan's life, she understands the physical feeling men must have upon seeing breasts. A warmth in her chest spreads out to her arms, down into her crotch.

He smells like pepper. And lemon. He's probably speared fish in clear ocean water.

Joan would have to admit it now, the pop-pop-pop-pop of automatic weapons that tinkles just above the music, infiltrating their frenzied, dancing group from outside, from somewhere. But the young man has a strong hand on the small of her back, and lets her lean her face into his neck as they waltz in the aisle, then the driver starts the engines and moments later they are driving, and before she knows it, the Islander guide is leaning across her lap, pulling the curtains apart to reveal endless ocean sky and stars. Soft white sand.

For a long time, Sally and Joan stand looking out over the water.

Let's never, ever, ever leave, Sally says.

Deal.

The next day, the women find their spots on the beach and stay there almost the whole trip. Baking in the sun, enjoying their flirtations and reading, when they're not at the all-you-can-eat. And not thinking of home or work. Not one bit. #freedom.

• • •

The first day back is always hard, they say, but Joan realizes Day 2 is worse. Day 1, you're seeing people after the big trip and showing off your pictures. Day 2, you're pulled back down into the lobster pot with the rest of them.

Day 3, Mr. Carny goes on the warpath. Apparently Sally's replacement messed up the employee payroll cycle, and now everything has to be entered into the system manually. Joan avoids Sally's desk, grabs her coffee and the morning newspaper, and heads back to her cubicle to pretend to work. Everyone keeps complimenting her on her newfound glow.

Joan settles at her desk. The headline on the front page reads Family Gunned Down. A picture of the child, a mother, and a father. How they came through No Man's Land, hoping to slip through the border to a better life. What it must be like to live in a place like that, Joan thinks. She thought the Islanders were very nice, indeed. What a sin.

Her phone rings, and it's Sally, asking for help.

Sighing, Joan folds the paper and puts it in the recycling. Sally is having a bad enough day already. She gathers her coffee, and prepares for reality.

RUSSIA

RUSSIA

RUSSIA

IN THE DREAM, MOTHER WAKES me late at night. We meet my father and brother in the foyer and pull on wool coats, winter boots. Mother tucks my hands into mittens and my head into a hat. She ties a scarf around my neck. We head down the front steps and walk into the forest at the end of our street where the trees sag under the snow's weight. It is cold with the kind of frost that materializes at your mouth in tangy shards. Mother walks between us, my brother and I, holding our hands. Father walks ahead. I watch the trees, hopeful for animals. None appear. Instead, pinned to the trunks of trees are paintings.

Mother, I ask, and I am speaking something Slavic, why are there pictures?

It's to hide them from the Germans, she says.

We come to the clearing where people have gathered, children mostly and school teachers. Suitcases sit in semi-circles. Dmitri from my class waves hello. He is hugging a vase.

The adults gather around a man, a stranger, and we

cannot hear. When our parents turn back to us, they are somber and strict.

You are going with this man, they say. You will be safe with him.

And then they kiss us goodbye, me first and then my brother. They join the other parents who disappear in twos and fours. I give chase, but the stranger is quick behind me. He takes my shoulders and tells me I must let them go.

• • •

Thursday night the knitters meet. When it gets slow, I take out my book and read behind the counter. During this week's meeting, I finish the *Vagabond's Guide to Travelling the World* and it occurs to me that, if I'm going to travel, it would be best if I knew how to swim.

The next morning, I sign up for lessons. Tuesdays at seven, paid for with money from my travel savings. After I am registered and get the tour, I take a bus to the mall and a painful three hours later find myself at the checkout with a passable bathing suit and a beach towel that has a picture of a beach towel and a beach ball on the front.

In the evenings, my mother asks me questions.

What are you doing with all of the books?

I told you.

Told me what?

I'm going to Russia.

Pfft, she says. What is it with you? When will you grow up?

I've been saving money.

C'mon, now. You won't be able to afford that. Not with rent and bills and the car payment. Honestly, she says,

I don't know you appreciate anything.

I watch her take the bottle into the living room and pour a glass, turn up the TV. I follow her in, take a seat on the couch.

Russia is known for its vodka, I say. I bet I could bring some back for you.

Hmm, she says into her glass. That would be nice, honey.

• • •

One large double-double and a tea with one sweetener…no, not that kind, the blue kind.

It's a wet Tuesday and the customers come in reeking of one thing or another. Wet cigarette smoke. Wet dog. Wet night downtown. They line up politely, hugging the wall to the left.

That's $3.50.

Wet Dirty Socks pays and moves to the right. The clock says 9:12.

Four medium double-doubles and one black, one sugar, says Wet Unidentified Ointment. Do you have any cinnamon rolls?

No. All out. Sorry.

What about cheese Danish?

All out.

Regular Danish?

Somebody opens the door to accommodate the growing line. There is a to-do, and Wet Dirty Socks is up by the counter again, his coffee knocked to the floor by accident.

Sorry, I say. We don't carry regular Danish.

Oh. Ointment says and kind of snorts and the manager is behind me right away.

The lineup watches. They are caffeine free and that's bad. I'm not a coffee drinker but I know that's bad.

I feel the manager's eyes on the back of my neck. He thinks he senses the possibility of a slip up. He wants to write me up in his little book like he writes up the baker every other day. I take a deep breath.

I'll have a donut, Ointment says. Plain.

I reach into the tray with a waxed-paper hand and extract the donut. I hand it to Ointment with a smile and Ointment smiles back. The manager moves on.

Will that be all?

Yes.

• • •

Mother has supper waiting when I get home. Cooked ham and a boiled potato that crumbles dry against my fork. She has been to the dollar store and to the mall with Celia and won twenty-five dollars on scratch tickets.

After the dishes, I go for my walk. St. John's is still beneath an oppressive fog but it's a nice, misty evening. I stop in the alleyway and listen to the music that drifts from an open bar door. When others pass, I pretend I'm looking through my pockets for cigarettes and then a girl gives me one and stands there with me so I am forced to smoke it, choking down each inhale quietly. She says her name is Felicity. She likes the band, and songs about the sea. Her brother died at sea, working. She hiccups and cannot stop.

Then she is gone, running to meet friends.

The puddles make a pleasant splash under my feet, each step fresh on the just-washed streets, so I take the long way back to the apartment.

• • •

I meet him behind an office building downtown. As I walk towards the car, I try to look sexy. I know I probably just look comical.

Out of habit, I put on my seat belt and buckle it at the side of my hip. He laughs and shuts the engine. He's not so bad looking. He seems kinda nice. But when he unzips his slacks and pulls it out, it's hairy in a way I don't expect and bulbous and fat. I can't help but screw up my face, not that he's paying attention. He's leaned back into the headrest, eyes closed.

No talking, please, he says.

I think of all of the women in books who sold their services for money or fame or to get out of a bad jam, and then I think the blowjob could not be part of this scheme.

I am just a mouth, I am repeating in my head.

I am just a mouth.

• • •

She smells of perfume, salt water.

A green tea, large, and a toasted plain bagel with low-fat cream cheese, she says, and—Jesus, as I live and breathe, Carrie, is that you?

I see that the woman at the cash, Salt Water Perfume,

is Terry Burns. Terry from seventh grade who lived on Ricketts Road. We shared a bunk in summer camp. I fumble with the bagel slicer.

Yes, I say. It's me. Hi.

Wow, she says. She gives me a good look over. She taps four perfectly manicured nails on the countertop, pattern of bored secretary. It's been so long.

Terry is in advertising. Terry is married and has two children with Brian Hensen.

Who is Brian Hensen? I ask and Terry tosses her hair, near professionally.

He grew up in Toronto. He's a solicitor. Just made partner at his firm.

My manager gives me the make-it-quick look, the don't-talk-to-customers look.

A lawyer?

Yes, Terry giggles. A lawyer.

Your bagel, I say and I hand her the small paper bag. She doesn't break eye contact. She snatches it out of my hand, brushing against my little plastic food-service gloves.

I'm going to Russia, I say, and it comes out just like that, too fast, before I can think. It hangs awkwardly between us, above the plexiglass counter and the cheese and meat and tuna mixed with mayo.

Russia? Terry says, and my manager clears his throat behind me. The queue is growing and Thomas, who is at the cash, is looking overwhelmed.

What's in Russia? Terry wants to know.

Adventure and intrigue, I say, and Thomas at the cash snorts and I wish I could will myself to shut my mouth already, what is wrong with me.

It must be expensive, Terry says.

Yeah, I say. Definitely.

Terry leans in then. I can see her nose hairs. She smiles white gleaming teeth. Well, she says, it was really nice to see you, Carrie.

There is a last whiff of perfume and she is gone from the store, disappeared into curtains of rain. Wet Caplin moves to the register and drops a handful of change on the counter, dimes and nickels and pennies that go flying off in every direction.

Small double-double, he says.

• • •

The first lesson is hard. The bathing suit does not fit as well as it did in the store, and I'm cold and wet from the shower. By the time I make it to the pool, everybody else is in. The instructor says she will wait for me. They watch my clumsy descent into the pool. They're probably blinded by the stretch marks, how they catch the light, pale blues and purples, the way the crotch of my bathing suit balloons when it hits the water. One girl giggles to her friend and when they think I notice they pretend to talk about something else.

I can't put my head under water. No matter what. I suck in a few cups of chlorine and come back up sputtering and retching, tears in my eyes. The instructor, Wanda, gives me special attention and after a million tries I manage to keep myself down there for a full ten seconds. When I break the surface, Wanda is laughing and clapping and I realize it is just us in a room of white tile and diving boards.

I shower alone but I keep the suit on, peeling it off at the end and toweling off quickly. I'm half clean and half chlorinated as I pull on my clothes. The clock in the dressing room says 8:10. The bus home is forty minutes.

I tell Mother about Terry Burns and her perfume. She says Terry was always a know-it-all, even as a young girl, and not to worry about it.

You're doing fine, mother says.

The clock chimes eight on the wall and mother says it's time for her show. I help her clear the table and she takes her tea to the living room.

Solicitor, I hear her snort to herself before the TV fires to life and the electric jolt of static blares across the living room.

I have time for some reading, then bed and then rain and work and rain.

• • •

This guy turns out to be my neighbour. By the time we both realize, I am in the car and it is too late. For a few minutes, we just look out the window at the gulls picking their way through the dumpster by the church. We consider the situation, but then he makes a comment about it being extra dirty this way. I have seen his wife and she is nice enough and pretty, so I don't understand but it's not for me to ask. He just wants a quick cowgirl in the front seat, nothing complicated.

Do you have a boyfriend, he asks when it is over. I am

smoking a cigarette in the passenger seat, I'm back on them full time now, and I shake my head no.

The smoke backs up in my lungs and I start to cough. It's dry and hacking and hard on the throat.

He looks out the driver's window and takes a long haul on his Marlboro. He tosses the cigarette out the window and turns towards me, as if thinking about it for a moment, then he asks if he can drive me home. The next morning I see him leaving for work with his briefcase and his three-year-old daughter in a car seat in the back.

Good morning, he says.

• • •

Three weeks. Three weeks. He has been repeating that all morning, whenever he sees me pass.

Devin. Do you think Miss thing here deserves to have three weeks off?

Aw, give it her, b'y. She's as good as gold, Devin says, winking at me.

I never got boys like Devin. I never got boys at all. I was born plain and quiet. You make peace with it early. Sometimes I wish I was more Jackie, with her hourglass figure and high-heel boots, but I can't imagine what it would be like to walk around looking like that all the time, getting all that attention.

That morning I had finally gotten the nerve. I walked right into the manager's office and I asked, in the loudest voice I could muster, for three weeks off in June. Before he said anything, I said I had worked there for five years and had not once called in sick and had not once taken any vacation. He nodded and said he would think about it. He said he was taken aback by my forwardness, so I left him there to think and went to put on the morning coffee. I find myself sick to my stomach and have to run to the bathroom and this keeps happening. Once in the middle of a long coffee order from one of the office girls.

I wouldn't say gold, he is saying to Devin now, but Devin is not listening. The manager is staring at me, sizing me up. He is deciding whether he will help me or not, but we close for the evening without final word and it goes on like that for the rest of the week. I lose six pounds.

• • •

I dream that I am running through St. Petersburg and I am covered with orange peels and banana peels that were dumped from a window onto my head. There is a snow globe snowfall. I am running through the streets and buildings and finally I reach a bridge that is haunted. The ghosts are right there, drifting visibly, a half-dozen of them. When they see me coming, they start to move towards me. They are flying. I see on the railing that somebody has left a coat. It's the most beautiful coat I've ever seen.

When I try it on, I disappear.

• • •

I think you should talk to the parish priest, mother says.

I have made her the cabbage soup, and she thinks it's awful. She doesn't know how I will sustain myself in Russia. No man will take care of you there, she says. You will be lost or raped or worse.

She shakes her head disapprovingly.

You must not go, she says.

Father Sean appears at dinner on Sunday. He wishes to talk me out of it, and asks my reasoning. Leaving home, he says, is a big decision. I tell him what I've learned about Russian history and he tells me about Trotsky and Dostoyevsky. I tell him about the cities and towns and their streets and show him the maps I ordered from *National Geographic*. I tell him about the network of hostels and the Lonely Planet guide. I could get a job in a café.

Do you speak any of the language? he asks and I tell him the words I know, which are slow but I'm getting used to them. I've been practicing around the house using a tape from the library.

We go over my financials. I will have enough to get there and live for two months before I have to find work.

Mother says supper is ready and we meet her in the dining room and sit around. He says he is satisfied that I am prepared.

Pass the cabbage, he says, and mother bows her forehead to the table in deference to his decision.

• • •

On the sixth lesson, I let go from the edge and I swim three, four body lengths before I panic and begin to sink. The water floods my nostrils and my mouth and my lungs fill like balloons. Wanda is pulling me to the side, I think. Somewhere off in the distance I hear her saying, don't fight me, don't fight me.

I am lying near the pool and there seem to be a lot of eyes. I cannot see the faces for the eyes, unblinking and worried. Soon they move back and it is Wanda and one of the girls from swim class who stay with me and get me to the locker room. Wanda tries to peel off the suit before holding me under the spray of clean water but I protest for her to leave it on.

She is saying, you did it, you swam! You did it, you swam!

● ● ●

There are shots to get and I will need to pay up front.

What is in Russia? Devin asks as we load in the crates of milk.

All kinds of things, I say. Architecture. History.

That's a lot of money for shots.

You need them when travelling like that, I say like I know.

The manager comes to my locker at the shift change. Your three weeks have been approved, he says. Congratulations.

I wait a week to tell mother. She says fine. She says go ahead, do whatever you want. She says she has tried to give me everything.

● ● ●

He's sitting in a blue Datsun at the end of the church parking lot. I walk to the car like I'm meeting a friend, and take my place in the passenger side. He lights a cigarette and says nothing for a while. We watch two women descend the stairs, probably just out of confession.

Show me your tits, he says.

I feel a tingle go through my whole body. I unbutton my shirt and the cool February air rushes in and makes my nipples hard. I wonder what he thinks of them.

He puts his hands in his pants and he moans. He stares at them like they're not part of me, as if they are mounted on the dashboard. It seems rude to turn away, so I watch until the hot liquid squirts a thin stream across his T-shirt and his breath catches.

He takes a wet nap from the console. I button back up.

So you work at Joe's, he says.

Yes.

How would they feel about you wearing their uniform for a thing like this?

I shrug and watch the starlings flit across the asphalt.

He closes his eyes and we stay there for a while. Then he says reach into the glove compartment and pull out his wallet. When I do, his registration falls out too. His registration says Brian Hensen.

Brian Hensen hands me a hundred dollar bill.

Thanks, kid, he says. You made my day.

I stand there for a while watching the cars on the road below, trying to figure out where to change a hundred. Wondering what even is the difference between a lawyer and a solicitor.

• • •

I am officially a swimmer. I can doggy-paddle, breaststroke

and float on my back without fear of sinking. The butterfly will need some work, but I should be able to get around in water, should I find myself there. There is a certificate that Wanda hands to me personally. It was challenging, she says, laughing, but I knew you could do it.

I fold the certificate in half again and again until it is small enough to fit inside my wallet. You never know when you may need to show your credentials.

There's a talk about post-Stalin Russia at a fancy bar downtown that serves martinis and other cocktails that people only drink in the movies. I worry that beer will make me seem too masculine, and I'm not sure what's in a martini, so I order a screwdriver.

The lecture is delivered by a young professor in a tweed jacket with patches at the elbows just like on television. I stand in the back and all the words seem magical. He knows so much. I cannot wait to be there.

A man who stands next to me says he is from Russia and has the accent, too. I tell him I'm going. He says, Godspeed.

• • •

I dream that I am travelling in a small car with four others along a dusty mountain road, high up in the cool air. We stop at a gas station in a small mountain village and while the others rush ahead, I am stopped by the northern view. On the horizon, beyond the forested mountains, are spires and onion domes ringed in tangerines and aqua-marines, golds and silvers. They stand sentinel against clear blue sky.

But first, a deep ocean. Mama, you would be so proud. I take off my coat, stuff it into my waterproof backpack. I peel off my jeans. I reach into my pockets to clear them out first, and pull out a ticket for a free coffee, ripped from a paper cup.

I fling the little piece of paper into the air, watch it leave on the wind.

I say to the others: watch this.

I dive.

WHITE CAT

WHITE CAT

WHITE CAT

THIS CAT HAS BEEN COMING around, I say to Jean and she nods like of course it has. It's been coming around and I can feel it watching me through the window sometimes when I am sitting at the table. It gets up on the deck and then the back of one of the outdoor chairs and it sits and watches me smoking and reading. Staring is more like it. I've gotten used to it, I suppose, but it's more than that.

Jean tosses her hair. She has a spray tan and she is ordering the salad.

I've named him White Cat. It's because he's white, really. Though he's so dirty he's almost grey. He's been outside for a long time.

I first saw him wandering down the hill about a year ago, just after I moved in. Then I saw him on a neighbour's porch and sometimes outside the store, waiting for scraps. I think he belongs to everyone, this cat. Though I've never seen him interact with another person. He conducts his business in private. He's of the earth, like. He knows where to hide and how to get around quickly. Though I think the new condo development might have displaced him. He's skinnier and dirtier than usual. And of course, I'm feeding him.

Of course, Jean says. She orders a glass of white wine. Not the most expensive wine, but the third from the top. She likes her wine German.

I've been thinking of getting him fixed and taking him in. I'm not allowed, but the way he keeps coming around. It started in the fall. I'm very worried about him. When it rains or snows, he does not come. No shelter in my yard, you see. He must have some other place. I worry it's a dark place, you know? And cold. I've spent nights up listening for him. When I would hear the snowplow on my street, I would imagine him getting crunched into a snowbank, freezing to the death, all broken up. It caused me such distress. I would stare at the ceiling. When I shovelled the car out in the morning, I was sick with the idea of coming upon him like that.

One night, I went out looking for him. I couldn't sleep anyway. I hauled a coat and boots on over my pajamas and went out on the street at 3 a.m. and walked up and down, making that sound that cats come for and carrying a slice of ham. He didn't come.

If he survived the winter, probably he's okay now, Jean says. She is making a point. The waiter brings the wine in a little glass canister.

Probably, but I can't be sure. He's on his own out there. He might have been somebody's cat once. He seems to know about humans and houses and such. All that staring. It makes me think he wants more.

White Cat follows a specific path over the stones when

he creeps up through the garden. He does not walk the grass. This is the way he always goes. Cats are suspicious creatures, you know. White Cat has his own way of doing. He takes each pellet of food out of the bowl and drops it on the ground before eating it. This goes on for a long time. If I'm standing outside watching him, he will not eat. He eats immediately when the door is closed. He doesn't mind me watching from the window. I get a cup of tea and sit on the counter.

Jean laughs. She says it's time for a smoke and we leave our table with our coats on the chairs and smoke on the sidewalk by the door of the restaurant. Jean tells me about work that day and how she wants to go to Toronto in the summer.

Back at the table, she says you don't need a cat. C'mon, she says and tilts her head the way she does. She has earrings and I didn't know her ears were pierced. You know this, she says, and her earrings are hanging silver threads that knock against each other as she moves.

I do know, I guess, but it feels wrong to leave him out there. He's everywhere I look these days, trying to make a difference. Jean thinks animals are little furry machines that hunt and eat and pee all over your house. This is what you're taking on, she says. But White Cat is different, I think. He might need somebody.

The chicken is dry. Jean pokes through her salad, picking things out. She is stacking bits on the corner of her plate.

It's going to cost a lot, she says.

I know.

Last night I fed him and he stuck around for a while

after. I stared out the window and he stared back in at me. It grew dark until I couldn't see him. I went to turn on the patio light and he was gone. Maybe he'd been gone a while. I wasn't sure. Then the phone rang and it was my mother. She said come over to the hospital and bring Dad some oranges.

I'm so sick of going to the hospital. You sit around in waiting rooms and drink bad coffee and eat stale chips from vending machines. The bags are half the size for the same price. My mother stays close to him in the room, and always goes in first, so I have to wait my turn. Do you know what waiting rooms are like? It's the dregs of society. It's everybody, all at once. All social order breaks down. There is blatant staring and eating with your mouth open. People cry or play loud games on handheld devices or talk on cellphones. Kids are running and screaming. It's worse than a trip to Walmart. But I went anyway. Mom brought Dad the oranges and I grabbed a bag of chips and pulled the plastic tab back on my coffee lid and settled into a chair in the corner. I read three magazines. I came across an article on forgiveness.

I eat the chicken and the potatoes slowly while Jean looks at me.

So what will you do? She says.

I'm not sure. I suppose I could take him in for a night, see how he makes out. He might cry and disturb the neighbours. I could call the vet and get a quote.

The waiter is sniffing around the table. Jean orders another canister.

Hmm, Jean says. Let's go for another smoke, she says.

We order dessert and coffee and take our coats.

We smoke on the sidewalk by the door. There is a light rain falling; water on Water Street. Jean shields her hair with a hood. She draws her coat in around herself and shivers. It's a damp old night, she says.

THE LOTTERY

THE LOTTERY

THE LOTTERY

GREGOR LEANS INTO THE BACK of the bedroom door, wiggling her legs. The only way is to shake your shoulders back and forth. Not that she has shoulders any longer. She is Gregor and she is too early. She can scuttle, skitter and hiss. The hissing was hardest. She sounds nothing like the track she downloaded but then maybe that's okay. She is sexy Gregor.

The clock ticks, tocks past seven. Five after. Ten after. Quarter after. She is sweating in the neoprene suit. A bead of perspiration starts a slow ski down the back of her neck that she cannot reach. She presses her back into the wall, moves up and down. No luck. The key turns in the lock at 7:20 and she drops to the bedroom floor.

Gregor moves into the centre of the hall.

Ross drops a stack of papers, yells something unintelligible.

Gregor suppresses laughter and scuttles towards him, skitters back. She hisses like she learned. Then she lifts herself off the ground, feet forward, and manages a hip bump in the oversized red lace panties she has taped to cover her crotch. Well, Gregor's crotch. You know, if cockroaches have that.

Ross is red-faced and laughing. Yum, he says, half-heartedly, kicks off his shoes. She drops slowly and awkwardly, not like a bug would drop, and skitters slowly backwards and forwards in the hallway, shaking her shoulders to wiggle the legs. She catches on the telephone table as she attempts a turn and the papers she has placed on the edge come fluttering down.

Gregor flees to the room, apparently alarmed, and hides beneath the bed, hissing.

Oh, Gregor, Ross calls. Where have you got to, Gregor?

She can see him through the bed skirt, pulling off his black sport socks. She inches a little ahead, her antennae visible against the material.

He is unbuckling his pants, taking them off, laying them across the chair. Come on out here, Gregor, he says. I've got something for you.

Gregor scuttles halfway out and then back and then slides fully into the light, ready for her prize.

• • •

Every morning at eight, they go to the café. Ross has his coffee black and reads the national papers and Sidney reads whatever book she's been saddled with in class. There is a man, a regular at the café, who hoards the papers. He arrives early and snatches a few copies of each for his booth. He keeps them underneath his tray for safe keeping. When you go there often, and he decides you trustworthy, he will seek you out, alert you to his supply. It becomes that you walk past the table and he nods without looking and lifts the tray and you snatch your papers up without losing step. He keeps Ross's favourite paper on top.

Ross says he wants to see the book she was assigned.

Sure. Go ahead and take it if you want it, she says and he does. She says, this sandwich is fucked.

Fucked how?

The cheese isn't melted and it smells like rot.

It's eggs, Ross says. Eggs smell that way.

Sidney brings it back to the counter. She has to stand in line, even though. She asks for the manager.

They're going to spit in my food now, she says back at the table.

Sure, babe, Ross says and turns the page.

• • •

He liked it, Sidney says.

No way! That's messed.

Val signals to the bartender. Sidney has had four gin and tonics and it's just past seven.

Seriously. Four times liked it.

Wow. Man's got a serious issue. I wonder what that's called.

What?

Sexual attraction to bugs.

I don't know, Sidney says, but I'm buying the suit. It would be hard to bring it back now anyway.

Ugh, Val says. Just ugh.

Earlier they are walking and there was Ross, surrounded by a bunch of wide-eyed undergrads, spewing some academic wisdom. Mr. Rockstar. Sidney wants to stop and tell them he has bad habits. That he bites his nails and is really nervous and that his dick is not that big after all but as they move across the group, he looks up and he sends her a wink the giggling girls catch and they are jealous of her, she can see it. She tosses her hair and they look disappointed.

You're like royalty, Val says. Campus royalty.

Sidney smiles. Orders another drink. Checks her phone.

• • •

They go to the party as A Very Old Man with Enormous Wings and the woman who was turned into a spider. Nobody gets it. Ross's cannulae get stuck on a Happy Halloween banner and two of his students spend the better part of an hour trying to extract him. Everyone laughs at him, except the spider.

In class that morning, she watched the same two students fawning over him. They don't get who she is. Sidney wonders if she should stop calling him Dr. Filbert but he says no. When she moves to another class, maybe.

Ross, she says, half drunk on wine, have you unstuck yourself yet?

I see no Ross here, he shouts. Call me Gabriel! Everyone laughs appreciatively. Sidney runs her tongue over her lips slowly and Ross watches, cannot take his eyes from her.

Later, when they're fucking doggystyle on the living-room floor, Ross's wings too big to get through the bedroom door, he says, I bet the angel wanted to do this the whole time.

• • •

I'm always something small and squishable. I want to be something different the next time.

Be something different then.

What will I be?

Whatever you want.

It's never about what I want, Sidney says, and the coffee burns and she shouts and the other customers are staring. Ross points to a little note on the side, turns it around so Sidney can see it. It says Beverage Can Be Hot.

Ross wants to be the Book of Sand but then, he says, you can't hold sand. It will seep out, one way or the other.

On the way from class that evening, someone yells Professor Filbert!

The girl is tall and auburn-haired, Amazonian.

He stops and lets Sidney move ahead, so she walks all the way to the car without stopping then stands in the rain until he catches up. Every drop of water a punishment. It is so her books and her clothes are sopping.

What are you doing?

Waiting, she says.

He towels her off in the foyer, still cursing about the wet seats. They don't speak at dinner.

There is a website where you rate your professors. Most of the comments under Ross's profile are that he is hot, that he is sexy, that he is hard to listen to because of his ass. Sidney sinks into her chair and reads the newest comments while Ross snores in the bed in the hallway. He wants to sleep alone tonight on account of his back. Someone has written did you see that blonde he is with. They are like the perfect couple.

• • •

Sidney has a pile of rocks arranged in the middle of the floor.

You're grasping at straws, Val says.

I think it's cute.

It's violent.

Maybe.

It's pathetic.

Fuck off.

It is, Sidney. It's pathetic.

It brings a whole new meaning to get your rocks off, Sidney says and Val laughs and Sidney says go on now, Ross is on his way.

He steps in the door around 7:00. He just stands there.

You want me to throw rocks at you?

Not really, Ross.

This is just weird.

I thought you liked Shirley Jackson.

Sidney takes the pile of rocks and re-arranges them in the living room while Ross gets undressed, goes off marking midterms.

You're just an associate professor, she says at McDonald's in the morning.

What's that supposed to mean?

Nothing, she says.

He fixes her with this look.

Nothing, she says. Go back to your marking.

EVERYTHING'S COMING UP
SYLVIA PLATH

EVERYTHING'S COMING UP SYLVIA PLATH

SHE SAYS SOMEONE IS GOING to die. A woman.

I look at the cards like I know what they mean. Nod my head. She taps a sharp fingernail on the ace. I roll my eyes.

It's rare that I see this card as death, she says. Usually it means change.

The fortune teller's brow furrows. I think she must be dying with the heat in all of those scarves so I get her a glass of water. She reaches into her purse and pulls out a worn plastic cigarette case.

A starling lands on the back deck, hops to the cat's water bowl and drinks. Imagine that life. Endless grass fields. Blue foam surf raking stones back from a beach, the ocean roar so vast it's the full of your ears. Salt spray on wings.

She says that this person who will die, all she puts into the world is negativity so it is all the world can give back. She says her negativity is eating her alive.

I think of the women I know, how they are struggling. It could be any of them.

The fortune teller lights her cigarette with a match and lets the flame burn until it is almost at the skin of her finger. The ashtray I give her was my grandmother's. It's green glass and smooth and heavy, the size of a dinner plate.

Oroboros, she says. The circle becomes complete.

The serpent eats its tail.

That night I wake to a creaking on the stairs.

I lower a toe to the floor, set it down silently, then the first foot and the other. I stand. I creep into the hallway and click on the bathroom light expecting men in masks or ghostly figures but it's just the cat sitting on the landing, licking his paws.

He follows me back to the bedroom and curls up at my feet. I wish I'd kept the money. Friggin' psychics. Not worth a dime.

• • •

Molly stomps in with those big old winter boots on, skirt barely past her ass, saying give me one of those lines in that saucy tone of hers. I hand her the book and she takes two in quick succession. She is the full of the stall and I'm pressed into the toilet tank, the condensation seeping into the right leg of my pants. Thanks, sexy, she says and twirls a few pieces of hair into place in the mirror and is gone back into the bar. I don't think she's ever bought a cigarette or a draw or a bit of blow in her life; a beer, for that matter. I've calculated her debt from these random encounters alone to be more than a grand, it's been going on that long. I take the final line myself. She's a cunt, that's what I think.

Al and Marcus are on opposite sides of my chair and they move to let me in. All straightened out are you, Al says and hands me my beer. I suppose I am straightened out. Everything is sharper. The speakers have lost the static buzz that pesters me most of the time. The door opens and the wind whips in and along with it, the final few that bring the place to capacity. Someone locks the door and suddenly there's a doorman and suddenly we're all a part of this world, like it or not, in it for the haul, me and Al and Marcus and Molly spouting off, high as a kite on my coke, on the other side of the bar, something about film. Listen to her going. It's one thousand and three hundred and twenty dollars, plus interest. I type it into my phone.

Somehow after all of this night and the downs and downs and false hellos and bullshit honesties, this is comforting. I have a seat and a drink and a full stomach and nose. Who we are is irrelevant. It's what song you put on the jukebox and who you're sitting with that matters or doesn't matter, depending on your take.

Take me home, Johnny, I say as soon as he walks in the door. I sort of yell it across the bar. He stumbles through the chattering groups, nodding hello. He's the type of person everyone is glad to see. Molly drapes a leg around him, tries to catch him as he passes. Somehow he's dismissive and friendly all at once. Everybody loves Johnny.

So what's this you're getting on with, he says. Somebody's going to die?

I nod, like: just wait until you hear this.

• • •

Julie works at the corner store, spends all day watching her soaps on a little TV in a top corner. Almost every afternoon I go up to have a chat and we eat frozen dinners behind the counter with plastic forks. The whole neighbourhood comes to the store. Julie knows everything that's going on.

You should have seen Stack Wilson, she says. Come in here the other day wanting cigarettes on tick. Just out, he was, and not a cent to his name. He's set up down by your place. You know, that yellow house on the corner.

I know the place. They drink all day and pile cartons of beer bottles on the front step. The cartons get wet and the paper crumbles off and it's towers of brown glass and some green, fading in the sun. They sell crack and coke out of the upstairs bedroom.

How's he looking? I ask.

Not bad, she laughs. You know, all built up from jail.

Stack Wilson is one of the boys we grew up with. Came to the neighbourhood late. We were fifteen or something like that, and all the girls were in love with him. Best looking boy downtown, they said. Could take care of himself too. A scrapper.

Maybe you should invite him for supper, I say.

Mind out, now, Julie says and laughs. Me and Stack Wilson.

Julie thinks we're washed up, old maids. She hasn't had a relationship in almost ten years and as far as she's concerned, Johnny is a lost cause. Probably Stack would come over for supper to her house. Probably he'd rob her blind, too. Leave her tied to a chair in the kitchen with her roast still browning in the oven.

I tell her about what happened. The prediction. I'm

wicked to do it on the one hand. On the other, it's a wonder I waited this long without blurting it out.

Jesus, she says. What if it's me?

We look around at the little store. The heater kicks in and makes a racket. She says what the fuck if I'm negative, ain't nothing to be positive about, is there?

She wants to see the fortune teller herself but it's twenty-five dollars.

You got me all freaked out now, she says.

• • •

Someone slips something slower on the record player. I take the joint from the fat kid next to me on the sofa. I'm Justin, he's said twice, but I'm still going to forget. The party is buzzing with full-moon madness. It's my last twenty dollars down the drain for a bottle of vodka and a two-litre of soda. I ask the fat kid if I can bum a cigarette, Justin.

This is what happens when you're high: air moves in waves. Add the spinning of too much vodka and it's like you're on a roller coaster that isn't quite moving but is moving too fast. In any case, you just have to ride that shit out. It ain't over til it's over kind of thing.

I don't know how I got here. Somebody's party in some house on Gower, but like every other party and every other house in this city. Like everything, faces everywhere that I know. Faces judging, asking me stuff. And all of this talk of death is bringing down my buzz.

Johnny comes to get me after his shift and we get some pizza and head to my place and put on Netflix. He tells me I'm getting ridiculous.

I think about the walk home, the fresh snow. Slush leaking through the wear in my boots. Winter was something to look forward to once, the air crisp and clean, GT snow racers and crazy carpets and wool caps that pulled down over your ears. The snow sticking to your mittens as you trudge back up the hill, trying to beat the boys. I was fast when I was young. A runner.

It's not healthy, he says. He takes my face in his hands and looks at me hard.

It's not healthy, I repeat.

That night I lie awake. The light from the laptop throws shadows that move on the walls. It's like someone else is with us, waiting.

I think of this and I have to get up. I stand in the hallway.

Who are you? I ask.

Johnny moans in the room and turns over in his sleep. Nobody speaks.

• • •

Leslie says give me a second and I stand on the doorstep for ten minutes before she reappears, hauling garbage bags. Just let me—she says and she heaves them around me and onto the lawn.

Come in, come in, she says. I'm just getting straightened away.

Do you need help?

Oh, no. You go ahead, she says, and she gestures to the table that's been cleared. She delivers a white plastic plate with crackers and hard cheddar cut in strips. The whole place smells like Lysol.

I watch as she pours the tea, how her hand shakes the kettle.

How are things? I ask.

Oh, you know, the same, she says. I have a new doctor. He wants to re-diagnose me. You know, based on what happened.

She says this and Warren's little face is right there in my vision. I can see him. I always imagine him bloody but I don't know, I wasn't there. There are pictures of him all over the living room, anyway. It's not like you could forget what he looked like. She rearranges them constantly, like she's trying to see something new. It's not a house so much as a shrine. I wonder if he's aging in her mind.

Post-traumatic stress, she says.

Makes sense, I say. I tell her about Johnny and that we're going to Montreal in a few weeks. I tell her about how he's getting on my nerves but I don't want to miss the trip. She says she likes him.

I really like Johnny, is actually what she says. It's on account of what happened with Warren, I guess, that she needs so badly to hold onto things. As if nobody can be left behind now. This is what I tell myself to account for her not being supportive, which I often find the case. It's not easy to lose a kid.

He's alright, I say. I don't know.

Okay.

It's probably not true, I say, and don't get all worked up but—and then I tell her all about the prediction.

Shit, she says. Who do you think it is?

I can't find words for some reason. I'm about to say it's not her and then she asks me point blank, do you think it's me, and her eyes go all wide because my mouth isn't moving. I'm thinking of what happened with little Warren and grief and how grief can do strange things, we all know that. But it was six years ago. But she's getting help.

She says, I think you should go now.

It's probably Jen, I tell her. She's been cutting again.

That girl, Leslie says.

I shouldn't have told you.

We're all friends here, Leslie says. Don't worry about it.

• • •

It's a long way up the hill to the house and my belly is full of alcohol. I don't know why I do this to myself. I can't get my mind off Jen. Called her house and she didn't pick up. Went over and beat on the door for half an hour and no answer before I gave up and went to the bar. That was five and now it's two and my socks are wet.

I smoke three joints before Johnny calls to tell me he's tired, he's going straight home from work, will see me tomorrow. For a while, I stand in the kitchen, looking out back.

The yard is full of good snowman snow, so I say fuck it, why not. Squat body, roundish head. Carrot nose, just like it's supposed to be. Rocks for shirt buttons. I christen him Fred. I ask him to dance. He says nothing. The sensor light on my neighbour's house comes on, and Fred is suddenly alive. I'm so glad to have company, I stay out there for a while. The cat comes back and I call him up to sleep in bed with me, so I'm not alone.

• • •

My sister nods and sips her coffee.

Why are you telling me this? she asks. I don't know why not. I'd want to know.

Do you think it's Lydia? I ask.

Pfft, my sister says, and then, maybe. Fuck. One of these days it could really happen, you know?

We move forward in the line.

Double mocha latte and one of those paninis, the fat man says. He pokes a finger at the glass until the girl gets the right one. He sizes up the sandwich as it hits the cash register, contemplating. He doesn't ask for more, just pulls out his wallet.

Nine dollars and eleven cents, the barista says. Huh. Isn't that strange. I catch my sister's eye before I reach for the phone. We are both dialing, just like that. A long time ago, we learned to listen to signs.

Fuck, my sister is saying.

Fuck, I am saying.

No answer. No answer.

We call Mom and she says a number on a cash register doesn't mean anything, Jesus, girls. Then she says Lydia hasn't been all that well lately, to be sure. Last time she saw her, she was really worried.

And this feeling goes over me like maybe this is it. And I can see in my sister's face that she feels it too. And nobody wants to be late to this kind of party.

On the parkway, the lights of my sister's SUV steady in the rearview. I'm weaving around the slow drivers. I'm honking the horn.

I swerve the car up over the lawn, and she bottoms out. I knock on the door. Then I knock harder. Let us in, Lydia, fuck's sake. My sister is behind me then, pushing me out of the way, sticking a key in the lock.

In the porch, the stench of garbage is liquid. I am through the cloud of fruit flies and into the kitchen when my sister stops solid and I bring up against her.

Aunt Lydia is standing in the hallway in a pale blue robe, her mouth agape. Her hair is up in a little white towel, white bony legs and bony arms all moving, gesticulating. What the fuck? she is yelling. You guys! What the fuck?

My sister slides to the floor, sobbing first, then laughing. I drop beside her, my knees weakened. I find myself starting to laugh too. It is a high, maniacal laugh.

You guys frightened the shit out of me! Lydia is yelling. Holy fuck! What the fuck is wrong with you?

She looks down at us for a moment on the floor then, stepping around, she heads to the sink and turns on the tap, fills the kettle.

Put your tea bags in this, she says, and she slides a little tray in front of us. She looks happy for the company. I'm sorry, I say.

It's foolishness, my sister says.

Hogwash, says Lydia, and snorts. The gashes on her arm from the last attempt glow white in the forty-watt bulb.

I smile and she smiles back and she says I ought to ask for a refund, that I've been taken.

That night, I lie with my eyes to the ceiling, taking in the blackness. On the ground floor, something creaks and it's not the cat, I've barred him out. It's just the wind.

I turn the lamp on and read a little of the book that Johnny recommended. I get to chapter three before I'm done with it and toss it aside. I fall asleep staring at the wall and I wake sometime later to a loud knock downstairs.

I sit up, not sure I've heard properly. My heart is a drum, stretching my chest. The house sits dreadfully still, the only light the dull amber of a small crystal lamp on the bedside table. There is only that light between me and the door and the staircase that would lead somebody from downstairs up. Some*thing*. My throat clenches, all of the moisture pulling back from my lips. I sit and wait for another noise.

Whatever it is, it sits and waits as well.

Through the thin windowpane comes the sound of a car barrelling up the street, then the screech of brakes. Somebody opens and shuts a screen door. Inside nothing stirs. Outside is entirely new to me, like it's coated in a fresh paint. Out there can save me, if I scream loud enough.

But there is no more noise. Eventually I get up and turn on the lights and do a sweep of the house. I find nothing.

• • •

She's at the Sunday flea market with a lineup, laying cards in sets of three. She's wearing the same rings and the same skirts, but the scarves have changed and there are more of them. Silks and satins, velvet lined, gold threaded, tartans and pashmina pinks. The lineup stretches all the way to the hockey-card table.

I thought I'd see you again, she says. I've been thinking of you.

Yeah, I was hoping you could tell me more.

She is shaking her head. She says there is nothing more to tell.

Can you see when, then? When it will happen?

I can't see that either, she says. Sometime in the year. I get the sense it is soon.

She lays the cards out, pushes my hand with the money away. It comes up again, the Ace. Same position. There is something else this time, she says. Family reunion of some sort. Before the spring, she says.

Nope.

No?

Nope, I say. I give her a five anyway, to be polite, and I head for home, feeling vindicated.

On the way to the house, I stop in the store and tell Julie all about it. Julie's gone to church and everything, is right religious. Confessed to a priest every year since elementary school.

That night I lie awake, have visions. Leslie plummeting off Signal Hill. Stack Wilson holding up the store where Julie works, beating her with a bat.

In the morning my mother calls to say Aunt Lydia is in the hospital, Fifth Floor, West 9. Psych ward.

• • •

If Molly even comes near me, I'm going to punch her out.

No need for that kind of talk, Johnny is saying. He is late for his shift at The Cardinal. He tells Al and Marcus to look out for me, to mind me, that I'm a bit off lately.

I'm sorry about the trip, doll, he says.

Montreal is off? the boys ask me, once Johnny is out of earshot.

Oui, I say. Financial interference.

Too bad, Marcus says.

I'm thinking now this is going to be the worst year ever. After everything, and now somebody is going to die, and no reprieve from this place and all these people who know me everywhere in this small town, on every street corner.

It's okay, I say. There's always next year.

I drink four beers and hear two bands and time passes fast, like it's sped up. On the way home, I decide to drop in on Johnny and let him know I'm okay. I get to the window at The Cardinal and take a peek inside and the place is dead, not like a Friday night should be. There is Johnny behind the bar, and there is Molly, the lone customer of the night, in a tight dress and heels, leaning in, telling him some funny joke. Maybe he'll take her to Montreal, I think. Fuck him.

When I get to the house, it's dark. In the morning, they tell me I didn't pay the power for two months and I tell them I'm sorry, that I was just laid off and waiting for the EI and looking for another job. Where have you applied? the girl asks me. Fuck you, I tell her. Pay in full or we don't restore, she says, and hangs up in my face.

I sit in the kitchen and look at the kettle I can't boil.

It takes me two days to take a concrete block from the construction site to the back of the house.

The wood in the patio is rotting, but I've searched and I've picked a good board, one that shouldn't fail. My toes curl around the concrete block. It lifts me just high enough to reach.

I tie the rope just like in the video.

I've locked the doors from the inside with heavy bolts, left instructions. I mailed the letter to my parents this morning. Packages by the door, I'd said, to be delivered to the girls and to Johnny. Sorry for the inconvenience.

But I just can't wait anymore really. All this worrying and waiting for someone to do it.

I unlatch one toe, then the other toes. The one foot, then the other foot.

A little bird drops from the sky and hops across the rotting patio boards to the water bowl and takes a drink. Soon the snow will melt.

The sun is high.

ACKNOWLEDGMENTS

Thank you to my editors, Kate Kennedy and James Langer, for their care and support. Thank you to Rebecca Rose, Samantha Fitzpatrick, and the entire team at Breakwater Books.

Thank you to my friends and family and to everyone who gave feedback, support, and encouragement during this process: Ryan Twiggy Arthurs, Daniel Barnes, Arabat Beowulf, Lenore Cahill, Mark Callanan, Bridget Canning, Brooke Davis, Nicole Durocher, Robert Finley, Donna Francis, Jessica Grant, Robin Grant, Valerie Hewitt, Joel Thomas Hynes, Peter Hynes, Andy Jones, Assane Kone, Sherri Levesque, Don Maher, Larry Mathews, Michael McCarthy and everyone at Glam Gam Productions, Carmelita McGrath, Bob Mersereau, Judy Moss, Paulette Murphy, Jenny Naish, Heather Paul, Tony Ploughman, Tamara Reynish, Margie Snow, and Liz Solo.

Special thanks to ArtsNL and the Writers' Alliance of Newfoundland and Labrador.

Versions of these stories appeared in *Riddle Fence*, *The Telegram*, *The Cuffer Anthology* (volumes VI and VII), *Paragon 6*, and *Newfoundland Quarterly*.

This book is dedicated to my father, Michael Waddleton, who told me I could be whatever I wanted to be when I grew up.

PRINCE ALBERT PUBLIC LIBRARY
31234900031103
Send more tourists, the last ones were d